DATE DUE		

SEP 0 8 2017		

Cover by Croco Designs
Formatting by Racing Pigeon Productions

There are always oodles of people to thank when it comes to writing a book, but this one was written while I was in the throes of some frustrating times. For that reason, I thank Janet Avants, Sara Bates, and Vinette Dicarlo for being thoughtful, supportive, and making me laugh in a wholly inappropriate manner.

AUTHOR'S NOTE

The First Dragon has long intrigued me—who was this mysterious demi-god who created the race of dragons? What did he do with his time? I knew a bit about him given his interactions with his son Baltic, but the rest of his life was a blank.

Until the day he started to talk to me. And then not only did he tell me his story, he urged me to stop writing the book I was at the time writing, and get to work taking down his tale. And since you don't ignore the First Dragon, I did as he demanded.

The novella you find here is part of the Dragon Septs series, falling after the events of Dragon Soul. I hope you enjoy revisiting the dragons—and watching the First Dragon face the modern world—as much as I did.

Katie MacAlister

DRAGON UNBOUND

CHAPTER ONE

The First Dragon was well aware of the noise outside the sunny room. The murmur of voices, both masculine and feminine, wafted up to him from what he knew was a stone-set patio below. But here, on the second floor in the small room with cheerful yellow paper patterned with turtles and reeds, the noise was muted, even though the window allowed in a soft summer breeze.

He moved past a lacquered dresser and a small bookcase bearing a carousel lamp and a telephone to the crib that sat near a window.

"Do you hear them, little one? The dragonkin like to talk," the First Dragon told the baby lying in its crib, its arms and legs moving to a rhythm that only the baby could hear. He leaned forward, smiling at the latest of his descendants. "It was always so. We are very passionate beings, and we share our feelings. Ah, you are a girl, I see. I am your ancestor. Your family calls me the First Dragon, for that is what I am. All dragons who ever were, and all who ever will be, are descended from me. You are part of a great heritage, child, one that most mortal beings know nothing about."

The baby blinked at him.

He considered her for a moment. He had a policy of telling new dragons just what traits he saw in them during his welcome visit. "You will not be blessed with the grace of your sister, but you will captivate males nonetheless. They will be charmed by your unique ability to see through illusion, and your fearless nature."

The baby gurgled up a spit bubble, her tight little fists waving about in a manner he found amusing. He touched a spot on her forehead, murmuring, "Blessings, child of the green dragons," before giving in to temptation and stroking her tiny pink fingers.

Immediately she gripped his finger, delighting him with her chuckle of pleasure.

"You are a little warrior, are you not?" he told her, oddly reluctant to leave this, the latest dragon to be born. "You possess your mother's courage and your father's intelligence. You will be a formidable enemy, and a stalwart ally. A very perceptive one."

The baby continued making gurgly chuckles, her fingers still holding on to the tip of his, her legs kicking out in that particular swimming motion that babies had. She had managed to remove the light covering laid over her, but given the warmth of the day, he was loath to put it on her again. He grimaced when she pulled his finger over to her mouth, and began gumming it, the wet saliva bubbles clinging to his skin.

"I must leave you, little one," he told her firmly. "I visit all newly born dragons, but I do not remain for them to chew upon me. I have many things of importance to do. I am the First Dragon."

The baby continued to mash his finger between her tiny, slobbery gums, unimpressed with his statement. Indeed, he had the feeling she was unimpressed with him altogether.

"Oh, very well, but only for another minute, as you are so determined," he said, resigning himself to having a wet finger. "I will admit this has been a pleasant visit to meet you. Of late, I find myself ..." He paused, frowning at the odd sensation that had gripped him the last few years. "Lonely is too strong of a word. Lonely implies a need, and I have no needs. Perhaps it is a desire for contact that I am experiencing. I wish to have more contact with ... someone. Someone who would talk to me. Someone who would care about me. Someone who—"

An explosive sound came from the depths of the baby's diaper.

He transferred his frown, which had been directed at himself, to the small dragon that gurgled delightedly before him. "I suspect what you have just done is not worth such pride, but I will take into account your age, and pass no further judgment. Farewell, newest green dragon. There may be a time in the future when we meet again, but if not, fare—"

The door opened on the word, causing him to take a step back from the crib. He wasn't startled by new arrivals, for he was the First Dragon. He never startled. But he was mildly surprised to find himself suddenly in the company of not just one dragon's mate, or even two, but three of them.

"The First Dragon!" the first mate cried upon seeing him. Aisling, he recalled, was her name. She was also a Guardian, if he remembered correctly, and he always did. "Eek! You're not going to do anything to my baby, are you? Because she's a dragon already, and she's cute, and she sleeps through the night, so I'd really appreciate it if you didn't do anything to her."

"Aisling," the mate named May said, elbowing the taller woman. "You can't talk to him like that. He's a god."

"Demigod, actually," said the third woman, moving forward. She gave him a steady look, one that always secretly amused him. Of all his descendants, this one never failed to stir emotions in him. Mostly exasperation, but there were moments, as now, when her spirit shone brightly and touched his soul.

"Child of light," he said, greeting her.

"Daddy-in-law," she said in a flippant tone that he knew was intended to irritate him.

He allowed one eyebrow to rise half an inch. "You are still annoyed with me, Ysolde?"

"Considering that I found you trying to convince my oldest son to allow you to make him a dragon when you know perfectly well that he's happy being a human—yes, I'm still annoyed. Baltic is furious."

"When is he not?" he couldn't help but ask.

Aisling giggled.

He looked beyond the women to the hall. No males had followed them. "There is a *sárkány*?"

"Not for a couple of days." Ysolde gestured to Aisling. "They're having a party to celebrate Ava's birth, and because half the wyverns are here for that, they decided to have a mini-*sárkány*."

"It's really more of a State of the Union than a full sept meeting," Aisling said. She looked with mildly curious eyes at him. "But I think the bigger question is, what is the First Dragon doing here?"

"I'd say interfering, but as you pointed out, Ava is already a dragon, so I have no idea," Ysolde answered. She gave him a pointed look that he chose to ignore.

Aisling *tch*ed in the back of her throat, and hurried over to her child, flinching as she did so. "Holy cats, Ava! You can't possibly be responsible for that smell!"

"You wouldn't believe the diaper shenanigans that Anduin got to before we got him potty trained," Ysolde said, still giving the First Dragon a gimlet look. "So, do you want to tell us why you're here?"

He lifted the other eyebrow. "Are you speaking to me, Ysolde?"

She winced at the little flicker of power he added to her name, and cleared her throat, but instead of backing down, tilted up her chin and challenged him with her gaze.

He sighed. "I greet all new dragons, and welcome them to the dragonkin. I have ever done so, and I will continue to do so."

"That's a thoughtful thing for you to do," said May, her voice soft and light as the wind. "But you look angry about something. You can't be mad at Ava."

"Child of shadows," he said, acknowledging May, mate of the silver wyvern. He had a fondness for her, too, since she had once formed the dragon heart from the shards given to each sept. "I am not angry at the babe. I simply do not like explaining my actions."

"You sure it's not something else?" Ysolde asked, tipping her head to the side while her gaze swept over him. "I'm thinking that you're not quite so happy as you claimed you were last time."

"Last time?" Aisling asked from where she'd been cleaning and diapering the baby. She looked confused. "What last time? The one in Egypt?"

"No." Ysolde gave him a long look, but he did not answer it. "He's been coming to see Anduin a lot. Well, twice. And then I caught him once with Brom, trying to convince him that he should be a dragon. And then Baltic said he saw him once, when we were out shopping. I think ..." Ysolde hesitated for a moment, her eyes softening on him. He smiled to himself. She had the tenderest of hearts of all his children, despite her definite lack of respect. "I think he's bored, and needs a girlfriend. Or better yet, a mate."

There was a collective gasp from the other two mates. He thought about rolling his eyes, but decided it wasn't an action of a demigod, and so maintained his usual placid expression. It had always stood him well when dealing with his sometimes fractious children, especially the volatile firstborn, those five dragons who had been born of his mates and gone on to found the existing septs.

"A mate!" Aisling said, coming forward with the baby in her arms, her eyes bright with excitement. "Of course! It can't be fun being all by yourself, and Ysolde said that Baltic's mom was one of your mates. ... Er ... how many have you had? Or is that a rude question to ask?"

He gave another little sigh, but no one heard it. "Some might say to address me in such a manner is rude in itself, but I will answer your question because I know that if I do not, Ysolde will continue to ask it."

Ysolde smiled, and the other women clustered around him. "You know me so well. Go on. What's the number? I'm guessing it's in the triple digits."

He allowed his lips to thin a little at her to indicate he was not pleased with such flippancy. "I have had two mates: the first was a minor goddess who bore me four children, the founders of the red, black, blue, and green dragon septs. Later, I took a dragon, Maerwyn, as a mate, and she bore Baltic and a child who did not survive the birth."

"A dragon?" Aisling asked, then wrinkled her nose. "I don't mean to sound disrespectful and all, but isn't that ... well ... incestuous?"

"She was six generations beyond my child," he told her, sadness leaching into his awareness. He had truly loved Maerwyn, which is why he'd taken her as mate. Her death left him bereft for centuries, during which time he had withdrawn from his dragons, withdrawn from everything.

May instinctively moved closer, and put out a tentative hand to touch the sleeve of his shirt. "Ysolde told us how Baltic's mother died. That was terrible."

He inclined his head in both agreement and acknowledgment of the sympathy she silently offered.

"That was, what, four hundred years ago?" Ysolde took his arm in hers. "It's time you moved on. And

I mean that in the nicest sense. Just because you're a demigod doesn't mean you can't be happy. Now, as it happens, this is the ideal time for you to be here, because as we mentioned, Aisling and Drake are throwing this party for Ava, and there's going to be a band playing tonight, and a *sárkány* tomorrow, and a bouncy castle in the side garden for the kids—which you probably won't want to be a part of, because they're loud little buggers—and basically all the dragons in Europe and a lot from other parts will be here, so you will have all the single ladies to look over."

"Yes, and we were going to have our Mates Union meeting now while the boys are downstairs guzzling dragon's blood wine, and the kids are out romping in the wading pool, but we'll just put the meeting on hold in order to take care of your business." Aisling put the now-stenchless baby back in her crib, and turned on a mobile bearing little dragons and jousting knights.

"What an excellent idea," May said, sitting cross-legged on the floor.

"Would you take this seat, Mr. ... er ... First Dragon." Aisling pushed forward a rocking chair, and seated herself next to Ysolde on a pink striped love seat.

"Hey, Ash, the kids went through the chips in record time and want to know when lunch is going down—holy shitsnacks! It's the First Dragon!"

The First Dragon, who had been contemplating the chair that Aisling had offered him, turned to eye the large black Newfoundland dog who marched into the room. "Ah," he said, noting several things about the dog, mostly the fact that it was not really a dog. "A demon. I had not realized the green dragons were in a state to require the assistance of a demon."

"Jim lives here," Aisling said, waving the dog to her feet. "It's mine, actually. I'm a demon lord, but I just have the one demon, and it doesn't do anything for us."

"Hey, now!" Jim protested, reluctantly marching over to its master, but pausing long enough to snuffle the First Dragon's shoes. "I do all sorts of stuff, not the least of which is entertain your spawn by giving them rides. And we gotta talk about that real soon, 'cause it's undignified, and if the other demons heard I was doing it, they'd give me no end of grief."

"We'll talk about it later," Aisling said with a warning glance at her demon.

The dog took a few whiffs of the First Dragon's trouser legs. "Hiya. Name's Effrijim, but everyone calls me Jim. Is it true you can make peeps into dragons? Not that I want to be one, because there ain't nothin' better than being a demon in Newfie form, but just in case someday Aisling completely loses her mind and starts acting like a real demon lord, it would be nice to know there are other options."

The First Dragon looked hard at the demon. Its eyes opened wide and it backed up to its master. "Man, I just asked! You don't have to look so scary. Ash!"

"You poke the dragon, you deal with the fire," Ysolde said calmly, pulling out a small notebook and pencil. "Right, let's do this properly."

The First Dragon weighed his options, and decided that his interest was piqued enough to remain. He sat in the chair Aisling had offered, and crossed one leg over the other, wondering just what the mates would do next. He had to admit, it was more entertainment than he'd had in a very long time.

"I call this meeting of the Mates Union to order," Aisling said in a formal voice, then added in a much more natural tone, "Jim, would you close the door? We don't want one of the men wandering up to accidentally hear us. Thanks. OK, let's see, we have stuff on the agenda, but we're putting that aside to deal with the First Dragon."

She cast him a quick worried glance. He tipped his head toward her and pierced her with a look.

"Or rather, to help him," she amended quickly.

"Way to piss off the head dragon," Jim said in a stage whisper to Aisling. "Now he's gonna smite Drake, or something."

"Quiet, you. And yes, that's an order. Unless you have something important to contribute to the conversation, and then you may speak. Honestly, Ysolde, you wouldn't believe the things Jim has taught the twins to say. They swear in Latin, they call Drake Daddy-o, and just yesterday I caught them trying to summon a demon to do their chores. ..." Aisling evidently realized that this was not the moment to continue. Instead she gave everyone a bright smile. "I turn the floor over to Ysolde, since the First Dragon is her father-in-law, and he's resurrected her a couple of times, so she knows him better than anyone else."

"Thank you, Aisling. Remind me to tell you later about how Brom is teaching Anduin the joys of dissecting roadkill." Ysolde gave a small cough, and continued in a businesslike voice, "Let us take stock of the situation. The First Dragon wishes to have a mate."

"As a matter of point, I don't believe I ever stated that desire," he said mildly.

"You don't have to," Ysolde answered, tapping the tip of the pencil on her lips. "You loved Baltic's mother, and you've been alone for several hundred years, and now it's time for you to find another woman with whom you can spend your life."

May raised her hand. "Forgive my ignorance, but can a demigod get intimate with a mortal? I mean, is it possible?" She made a vague gesture with both hands. "Can they ... er ... hook up?"

The First Dragon gave her a look that had her blushing beet red.

"Yes, well, I think we'll take it as read that everything is in working order," Ysolde said, making a note.

The First Dragon turned the look on her.

She ignored it, just as he knew she would. "But you bring up a good point, May. Immortality is going to be of prime importance. So, we have a limited pool of possibilities. I think the best way to tackle this is to get a list of the First Dragon's likes and dislikes."

"Smart thinking," Aisling said, nodding. "Who would you swipe right on?"

"Do you have a preference on hair color?" May asked.

"Do you like funny, or insightful? Walks on the beach in the rain, or curled up inside with a book and glass of wine?" Aisling asked.

"Are you into more athletic women, or homebodies?" Ysolde added her questions to the collection.

"And you're sure everything"—May did the hand gesture again—"will work OK? I mean, if it's been four hundred years ..."

The First Dragon stood up. "I believe that you all have good intentions, but this is intolerable."

"Why?" Ysolde asked, frowning at him and tapping the pencil against her lip again.

He was taken aback for a moment. Few beings had ever questioned him, and no dragons ... except Baltic and his Ysolde. He debated dismissing her question as not worthy of his attention, but decided that since she had a pure heart and a shining soul, he would unbend. "Even if I wished you to locate a female with whom I desired to spend time, you would fail."

"Oh, I do love a challenge," May said.

"Me, too," Aisling said, sitting up straighter. "Why do you think we would fail? You underestimate the collective power of mates. We're pretty good when we put our heads together."

"You would fail because if such a woman existed, I would have found her," he answered.

"You say that, but how hard have you looked?" Ysolde stood up and moved to within a foot from him. "You're never around in the mortal world. Except for popping in and trying to convince my son to be a dragon."

"You don't know what women today are like," Aisling said.

"Women have changed. So have the men, but mostly women have changed since the time when you were hanging out with mortals." May lifted her chin when he cocked an eyebrow at her.

"You're out of touch with the modern-day dragon, that's what it is," Aisling decided.

"And women of today! You have no idea what we like and want." Ysolde made another note. "Maybe we don't need to find a woman for you so much as you need to experience what modern life is like. Then, once you have a grounding in reality, we can take your wish list and help you find someone."

He considered whether he should be insulted, realized that they might have a valid point, and decided to see where the conversation led. He had forgotten just how entertaining it was to be amongst his kin.

"Excellent idea, Ysolde," Aisling said, giving her a thumbs-up.

"I agree," May said after some thought. "I think you won't connect with a woman of today unless you know what modern life is like. Therefore, you will have to stay here for a bit."

"Here?" Aisling said in a near squawk, her eyes widening. "Goddess! Well, I suppose he could have the St. George room, although that means booting Gabriel and May from it—"

"We'll be happy to move if it means helping the First Dragon," May said quickly.

"That's settled, then," Ysolde said, making a tick mark next to something on her notes.

"Nothing is settled," the First Dragon felt obligated to point out. "I have not agreed to your suggestion. Nor do I have any intention of doing so."

Ysolde gave him a long look. "You wouldn't be afraid of us, would you?"

His eyes widened at the brazenness of her comment. "You forget to whom you speak, child of light."

"Not in the least. I didn't mean to slight your courage, but I do think that perhaps you're hiding from the possibilities of finding another mate because of your memory of Baltic's mother."

"Which we totally understand," May added.

The other mates nodded and murmured platitudes.

"Even if that was true, I am the First Dragon," he said, allowing them to feel the weight of his words.

"That doesn't mean you don't have feelings like the rest of us." Ysolde smiled. "What was Baltic's mother like?"

He was mildly taken aback by the question. "She was gentle. She enjoyed embroidery. She had a great love of nature, and liked to weave in the garden quite a bit."

"Right. Crafty, nature girl, more crafty," Ysolde said, making more notes. "What else?"

He rummaged through his memories. "She was very social. She loved to have kin visit. She once said that without dragonkin, she felt lost and alone."

"Extrovert," Aisling said with a nod. "So no bookish introverts for you."

He allowed a little smile to escape. "She definitely was not one for books."

"That gives us something to go on," Ysolde said, and the other mates nodded their agreement. "We can start looking right away."

"I am the First Dragon," he reminded them. "I have existed for centuries without a mate. There is no reason I need one now."

"Uh-huh." Ysolde looked thoughtful for a moment. "How about if we put this in terms of a wager? We, the collected mates of your wyvern descendants, are willing to place a wager that you cannot stay in the mortal world."

"And live like a modern dragon," Aisling said quickly.

"And learn about modern women," May added.

"A wager!" He allowed them to see his disfavor. "I do not wager."

Jim the demon dog made chicken-clucking noises until Aisling swatted it on the head with a pillow.

"We wager you that you can't live like a modern dragon—modern wyvern—and get to know modern females of a dating age for a year," Ysolde said, the other mates murmuring their approval.

The First Dragon thought about his life, and unexpectedly found himself saying, "A day."

"Six months," countered Aisling.

"Two days."

"We will naturally settle on a month," Ysolde said with blithe indifference to the fact that his gaze was quite pointed. "You live here, with us, for a month. No magic, no demigod stuff, just be a normal dragon who meets and interacts with females like any other dragon, and at the end of that time, we'll know you well enough to find you a woman, or you will have found her yourself."

"That is not a wager," he couldn't help but point out.

"Not in the strict sense, no, but it is a challenge." Suddenly, Ysolde smiled, and he saw again why Baltic, his most fractious child, was so smitten with her. "And I don't think you're one to back away from a challenge any more than we are. Do we have an agreement?"

He thought for a few moments. Perhaps such an interlude would be sufficiently amusing to keep the increasingly frequent feelings of disquietude at bay. "Very well, I agree to your terms."

"Excellent," Ysolde said over the voices of the other mates as they declared their approval. "I think you'll find this will benefit us all. We'll get to know you better. You can see the children all you like, although to be truthful, I can't imagine why you would want to. Brom is going through moody teen years, and Anduin is a little terror, while Aisling's twins are—"

"Horrendous little monsters in adorable four-year-old form," Aisling said calmly.

"But assuming you *did* wish to see the latest generation, you can. And more, you will see how dragons fit into the world today." Ysolde's smile grew broader. "All the while we can be finding someone perfect for you."

He smiled a long, slow smile, one that said without words just how unlikely that would be.

CHAPTER TWO

"Are we there yet?"

I buried my head deeper under my jacket, and counted to myself. Five. That was the fifth time in an hour that Cassius had asked if we had arrived in the small Hungarian town where our next gig was. Five wouldn't seem like a lot, but it was when you were desperately trying to get some sleep, or risk losing the ability that paid your rent. I thought of pointing that out to the boys, but didn't want to get into another argument about why sirens needed to rest before pushing a crowd.

Starting with my toes, I made a concerted effort to relax my muscles, moving up my legs to my thighs, stomach, arms, and on up to my neck. By the time I was mentally chanting singsong meditative phrases, I was on the verge of sleep.

"Are we there yet?" Whomp. Someone kicked the back of my seat, instantly snapping me out of my relaxed state. I pushed off my jacket and sat up, snarling at Cassius's face, "I was almost asleep!"

"What?" he asked in his thick Austrian accent. A little sneer curled his lips. "You sleep too much. You are always sleeping. Every time I look, you are sleeping."

"No, I'm *trying* to sleep, something that's impossible with you knocking the seat around. Cheese and crackers, do you not understand how sirens work?"

"Oh god, now you get her going again," Rina said from the front seat, turning around to purse her lips. She was Russian, had red hair, and bore an insufferable expression that always made my palm itch. "Now we hear lecture of how to pull."

"Push," I said, sighing as I swung my legs off the van's bench seat, and turned to face front. "What I do is called a push, which you'd know if you listened to me instead of playing video games all the livelong day."

"What is livelong?" Rina asked, glancing up from her gaming device.

"It means you're always staring at that stupid Game Boy," Andrew answered, sending me a quelling look in the rearview mirror.

"Eh." Rina went back to her game.

I snarled a rude thing under my breath when Cassius jammed both feet into the back of my seat. "We better get there soon. I'm hungry. How much longer? I'm tired of being back here."

"Everyone has to take a turn in the back row," Andrew said, leaning one arm on the open window of the van as he drove. "Watch a movie or something. And stop fussing with Charity. You know she won't be able to distract the crowds if she's tired."

"Thank you," I told his reflection, and was going to lie back down on the seat when Cassius kicked it again.

"I'm tired of being back here! You stop and let me switch."

I knew I shouldn't have done what I did next, I knew it well, and yet, I did it all the same. I opened my mouth, and sang ten bars of an old English country tune, directing a push toward Cassius that would leave him in a subdued state.

Almost immediately, he topped over onto his side and lay motionless on the seat.

I turned back to find Andrew's gaze trying to catch mine. "Charity … ," he said warningly.

"Yes, I know, it's not polite to push bandmates. But I'm going to be dead tired tonight as is, and if you expect me to push a bunch of dragons, I simply have to get some sleep."

"Sirens shouldn't need sleep. You magic people with your song, is all. Why need sleep?" Rina asked.

"Because," I said, lying down as best I could on the bench seat, and yawning. "Our voice is just part of the element that bewitches people. It's the mental push that really packs a wallop, and dragons are notoriously hard to influence that way. Right, no wakies until we're in Hungary, please."

I went through my relaxation routine again and, this time, managed to actually drift off into sleep, not the normal sleep of everyday mortals, but the deep, energy-gathering sleep of a siren who was about to attempt a group brainwash of great a big herd of dragons.

"I'd like to know whose bright idea this was," I grumbled some five hours later when I stood next to Andrew, hooking up a microphone.

He nodded toward the massive house that sat smack-dab in an estate of what had to be at least forty acres. We were on the south side of the house, in an area that we'd been informed was once a bowling green and tennis court, but which now was serving as a stage. "How can you doubt that we'll come out of this rich as Croesus?"

"The dragon who owns that house might be rich, but you haven't been paying attention to your Tolkien if you think dragons don't guard their treasures against burglars," I pointed out.

He grinned at me in that cocky way he had. I toyed once again with the idea of getting to know him better, since there was something attractive about his fresh-faced Canadian self, but I knew in my heart it wouldn't work out. He wasn't what I was looking for in a man.

"And I think *you're* underestimating just how potent you can be."

"We've never tried this against dragons," I warned, pulling in the microphone cord. Andrew started arranging the sound board to his satisfaction. "They are notoriously hard to magic."

"But not immune, and just think of the haul we'll make here." He inclined his head toward the house again. "Even if it was just the owner, we'd make out like kings, but with forty or so dragons just waiting to have their pockets picked ... it fair boggles the brain."

"Just be aware that I make no promises about how bespelled they'll be." I set the mic at my preferred height. "Take it easy until we know they're not aware of what's going on."

"We will, but you remember that you have to keep them under for at least ten minutes. Fifteen would be better."

I shook my head. "Six songs is too much. I might be able to do four in a row, but five is beyond me. It takes too much energy. You've got eight to ten minutes, so use them wisely."

Rina stomped over to us, hauling part of her drum kit, and groused in her thick Russian accent. "Is too far from van! You should have driven here."

"And ruin this lovely lawn?" I rubbed the tip of my sandal against the velvety green lushness. "That would be a crime against nature."

"This better be worth it," Rina said darkly, giving me a look that I had no problem interpreting as a threat. "You put them under fast so we can take gold and leave."

"Gold?" I asked, shaking my head again. "You guys are nuts if you think we're walking out of here with gold. Do you know how dragons guard that stuff? Not to mention the fact that it's like an aphrodisiac to them, so they'd hardly leave it lying around. Let's just stick to the routine—I sing, Cassius picks pockets, and you two ransack the house for easily lifted valuables. Then we get the hell out of Dodge before everyone comes out of the happy sleepies I put on them, and discovers what happened."

"Pfft," Rina said dismissively, and began assembling her drum kit.

I rubbed my arms, and asked, "What's our name this time?"

Andrew consulted a piece of paper. "The Unequaled Moles."

I made a face. "Sounds unpleasant, but I suppose it doesn't matter since it will change after tonight's party."

"Speak of the devil," Andrew said, *tsk*ing at a long black electrical cord that had come uncoupled. "Here comes the lady running the whole thing."

I turned to where a woman with mousy brown hair trotted toward us, a large black dog on her heels. "Hi! I'm Aisling Grey. Are you the Uneven Moles?"

"Unrequited Moles, yes," I said, shaking the hand she offered.

"Unequaled Moles," Andrew said under his breath.

"Sorry, little joke. It's actually Unequaled. I'm Vicky, and this is …" I blanked for a moment on the name that Andrew had picked for this job. Part of the problem with special gigs was the fact that we used different names each time. "Er … Ernest," I finally got out. "The lady on the drums is Katya."

"Hiya. Name's Jim," the dog said, stepping forward and doing a quick gender check on Andrew. We both stared at it, and for a moment, I wondered if I was hallucinating. I'd seen many sorts of beings during the time our band had traveled around various Otherworld venues, but never had I seen a talking dog. "It's really Effrijim, but I prefer—"

"Jim, for the love of all that's holy, get your nose out of his crotch. I'm so sorry," Aisling apologized to Andrew. "It knows better than that."

"It?" Andrew glanced down at the dog and gave it a tentative pat on the head.

"I'm a demon. Sixth class, yet," the dog said proudly, turning its attention to me. "Aisling is my demon lord, but don't worry, she's not a bad one. Well, she's bad at being a demon lord, but not a bad person. Hey, babe! Gotta love a drummer, and a girl version is just made of awesome."

"May I remind you that I'm standing right here," Aisling said with a pointed look at the dog when it greeted Rina.

"Love ya, too, sweet cheeks," it said, grinning at her. I remembered that all demons were referred to using the "it" pronoun. I didn't understand why, but who was I to question tradition.

"Uh-huh. Don't you have somewhere else to go?"

"Nope. Love me some tunes, so I'm happy to hang with the band."

Rina climbed down to stalk over to us, her eyes narrowed on the demon dog. "You are demon?"

"Yuppers. Name's Jim. Hey, do you find all that drumming makes your boobs bigger? You know, like the 'I must, I must, I must increase my bust' exercises that girls do?"

"I don't know anyone who does that," Aisling said, swatting the dog on its head. "And stop being so rude. I'm terribly sorry, Miss … er … Katya. Jim's a bit deranged, what with the party and all the people here tonight."

"Is OK," Rina said, running her hands along the dog's back. Jim shivered in delight. "Demons I like. They are so very … *wicked*."

"Oh yeah, I'm all shades of wicked," it told her. "There's a spot on my back where if you scratch it just right, I turn into an animal, heh heh he—"

Aisling whomped the demon again. "And that's enough about your itchy spot."

"I'm just trying to be friendly," it said with a little pout.

Rina stroked it a couple more times, then leaned down and whispered in its ear. Jim's eyes bugged out a little, and it gave a low whistle when she returned to assembling her drums.

"I'm so sorry," Aisling apologized again to us. "But you know how it is with demons."

"Yeah, we're irrepressible," Jim said, turning its attention to me. "Hi there."

"Hello," I said, my palms pricking with a sudden dampness. I had no idea if demons were prescient enough to tell what I was. "I've never met a demon before. Is the dog form common?"

"Only for demons of extraordinary good sense," Jim answered.

"I'm so glad you're here. You wouldn't believe how hard it is to find bands who are hip to people in the Otherworld. If it hadn't been for the Otherworld Suppliers agency, I'd never have found you," Aisling continued, giving the demon a warning look. I wondered what I'd do if Jim suddenly started spilling the news that I was a siren. "This party was kind of a last-minute thing, what with Drake not wanting people around the baby, but she's almost three months old and isn't going to expire from all the attention. You're sure you can run those speakers out here? You have enough power? Not that I'm questioning your expertise, but I want to make sure that you sound … you know … *good*," she said, glancing at the speakers that Cassius was hauling by means of a hand truck. He hadn't fully come out of the mental push I'd given him, so was more docile and less bitchy than normal.

Andrew bristled slightly, but I gave his back a pinch before answering. "I know exactly what you mean— we've had those gigs where we weren't allowed to crank up the sound the way we would have liked to, but I assure you Andrew is an expert on sound equipment as well as being a hell of a keyboard player, so we'll sound just fine for your party."

"Oh, good. I'm so glad you understood what I was trying to say." Aisling gave us both a smile. Her demonic dog ambled over toward me, causing my breath to hitch in my throat. I was braced and ready for it to expose me when it gave my feet a friendly snuffle. Almost immediately it paused, and cocked a furry eyebrow at me.

"Hey." Jim took another sniff at my feet. "You don't smell right."

"Jim!" Aisling said, scolding the demon. "I'm so sorry, Vicky. Just ignore it."

"I didn't say she smelled bad—I just said she didn't smell right." It took a long, snorting sniff. "Like ... not exactly—"

"Aisling! We have a problem!" The cry came from behind us.

"—like not exactly human. Like—"

I braced myself for an outcry, but Aisling whirled around at her name, and moved a few steps to meet the woman racing toward us across the gorgeous emerald lawn.

"—like something not normal."

I tried frantically to think of what I was going to say when the demon revealed my true nature. "Don't be silly. What would I be if not human?"

Jim gave me a long look. "Dunno, but you're not a human like that guy beside you and that chick on the drums with the seriously kinky fetish about hairy black dogs."

A woman with a short black bob hurried up to Aisling, giving Andrew and me a little nod before continuing a bit breathlessly, "There's a problem with the First Dragon."

"Oh, god, what?" Aisling asked. "He hasn't changed anyone into anything, has he?"

"He told me he was going to turn me into a slug if I kept slobbering on his shoes, but I think that was just the way his sort shows affection," Jim said, leaving my feet to join its owner's conversation. "Also, Drake told him that he can banish me to the Akasha if I get what Drake calls lippy. Me! Lippy! As if! He can't do that, can he? Only you are supposed to be able to banish me, which I gotta say you do all too often. But still!"

"No one has been turned into anything, although Baltic looks furious that his father is here. I take it their relationship isn't the best," the dark-haired woman said.

"Well, granted, when your father is the same demigod who literally created the race of dragons, it can be a bit daunting to have him hanging around watching you, but Baltic can just get over it. Ysolde says he will, and look at Drake! He was horrified at first that we have this little wager going, but now he's resigned to entertaining the First Dragon for a bit."

"Resigned." The demon dog snorted. "Yeah, if

you call him threatening to take you and the spawn away and leaving everyone else behind as *resigned*, then I guess so. Hey, Vicky, are you a Wiccan? No? You're not a mage, 'cause you don't have that smell of arcane magic around you, and you're not a naiad, because I know all about what they smell like." It tipped its head at me. "May's twin is a naiad."

"May?" I asked.

The dark-haired woman looked over from where she had been conversing in a low tone with Aisling. "Oh, hello. Yes, I'm May."

"This is Vicky and Ernest. They're with the band." Aisling frowned. "What's the problem with the First Dragon?"

May glanced toward us. "Er ... I'm sure these people don't want to hear about it."

Andrew murmured something about it not bothering him at all.

"Actually, I've always been fascinated by you dragons," I found myself saying. "I think it's the juxtaposition of the traditional image of big, scaly fire-breathing dragons with people who look perfectly normal."

Aisling gave a short bark of laughter. "They may look normal, but I guarantee you they aren't." She turned back to her friend. "I don't think Vicky and Ernest care if we talk shop. What is going on with the First Dragon?"

May gestured toward the house. "He won't take our room. Gabriel is horrified at the thought that you gave us the best room, and the First Dragon should have to sleep in lesser accommodations. I'd say it was cute, but he truly is genuinely distressed. You know how he feels about honoring the First Dragon."

"All the wyverns do, even if Drake makes a fuss about having him here," Aisling said, pinching her lower lip. "They're so fusty and old-fashioned at times. Well, if he doesn't want to have your room, he doesn't have to. Lord knows this house has enough rooms that he can sleep wherever he wants."

"That's just it. He said something about sleeping in the gatehouse, I think. Do you *have* a gatehouse?"

Aisling gave a wry smile. "We do. Drake had it done up in case his mother ever visits. The First Dragon can stay there with my blessing."

"I'll go tell Gabriel so he can stop worrying." May flashed us a smile. "Nice to meet you. I look forward to the show."

Aisling watched her trot off to the house before turning back to us. "Sorry, guys—slight crisis. Where were we?"

"No problem," I said at the same time that Andrew asked casually, "You said there's a demigod here?"

"The dragon progenitor, yes." She made a face. "I don't think he's that bad, but the wyverns—those are the leaders of the dragon septs, if you aren't hip to dragonkin—are all aflutter at the idea that the head honcho has come down to the mortal plane for a bit."

"Indeed, that has to be a very great honor," Andrew said in a silky smooth voice that instantly made the hairs on the back of my neck stand on end. He was a true grifter, our Andrew, able to talk his way in and out of the most difficult situations. And now he was using that voice on Aisling. ... Mentally, I shook my head. I doubted if he would have the same effect on dragons as he did the others we had met in the last two years since we'd formed the band. "Will he be at the show tonight? I'd love to meet a real demigod."

"Who knows?" Aisling shrugged. "He very much gets to do exactly what he wants, and I have no idea if he's into music."

"Dude's been around a gazillion years," Jim said, eyeing one of the speakers. "Can't live that long without getting into *some* tunes."

"I'll invite him to watch you perform, of course, but beyond that, no promises. Jim, so help me god if you even think of peeing on that speaker, I'll send you to the Akasha and you'll miss the whole show."

"You're so mean to me," Jim said, but obediently moved away from our equipment. "I'm amazed you haven't given me a pee complex what with all the bossiness! *No piddling on shrubs, Jim. No pinching a log in the flower beds, Jim. Effrijim, I command thee to stop peeing on the leg of that stranger.* Sheesh! I'm going off to visit the little demons' room now, OK? And I might be a while what with having to work through my issues after you've stifled my creative peeing."

"Good," Aisling said, shooing the dog off. "Just make sure it's downwind and in one of the designated potty spots. Now, Vicky and Ernest, let's talk timing. Dinner will be at six, so if you start around eight, that should give us time to put the smaller kids to bed. ..."

Andrew, Aisling, and I spent the next five minutes discussing specifics, all of which were moot because we were going to do our own thing, but of course, I couldn't let Aisling know that.

Not for the first time, guilt pricked at my conscience, reminding me that what I was doing was wrong. I hadn't been raised to take advantage of people—far to the contrary. But that, I told myself as Aisling hurried off to her friends and family, was the path my life had taken once I discovered my secret talent. "And unfortunately, there's not a damned thing I can do about it," I said under my breath.

"About what?"

Dammit, I forgot that Andrew had such good hearing. I gave him a wan smile, and absentmindedly coiled up one of the cords that lay tangled behind the closest speaker. "Nothing. Just talking to myself."

He gave me a curious look. "You aren't thinking about backing out, are you?"

I did a good approximation of an astonished gape. "Are you kidding?"

"Because I know you were upset the last time." His gaze was a lot shrewder than I liked. "I told you then and I'll tell you again that we aren't hurting anyone. We only hit people who can afford to lose a bit of their blood money."

"You don't know—" I started to say, but stopped immediately, warned by the frown that suddenly appeared between his brows. I held up a hand and added, "Never mind. I'm not backing out."

Not now. Not until I found a way to escape them.

Dear goddess, I hoped I found a way, because I wasn't sure how much longer I could do this without either burning out my brain or killing my soul.

The problem was that the alternative—hiding in the seclusion that I'd been in for more than ten years—was unbearable.

There had to be another way. I just hoped it wouldn't be the end of me.

CHAPTER THREE

If your thoughts were as clear as your eyes, and the whole of your heart were true.

I picked the man out the second his foot hit the grass. We were well into the third song of the set, and Andrew's program running on the laptop that sat on his keyboard had switched the big lights from us to the people dancing on the grass in front of us, in kind of a low-budget approximation of the lights in a club. With the brightest of the lights out of my eyes, and from my elevated position on the portable stage, I saw a man emerge from behind the ten-foot-high hedge that segregated this section of the garden, and stroll over to the back of the crowd of approximately fifty people.

If your pulse beat time to love as fast as you think and plan.

This man was tall, taller than several of the people at the back, with a silhouette that wasn't bulky, but wasn't thin. He had dark hair with a white stripe on one side, and the way he moved reminded me of one of the big cats that lived at a zoo in which I'd taken shelter for a few weeks. Most of the cats were nervous as hell around me, but one, a black panther named Leon, didn't seem to mind my presence. This man reminded me in some intangible way of Leon ... or at least, of the way Leon prowled through his Amazonian exhibit.

If you felt as much as you thought, and dreamed what you seem to dream.

Given our distance, I couldn't see his eyes, but I felt his presence as if he was Leon ... strong, silent, and filled with a secret power that his prey saw only at the last moment of life.

These days, half-sweet and half bitter, would taste like Olympian wine.

At first the man was watching the crowd, but suddenly he turned to look at me. Here's the thing about a siren's song. ... Even when we aren't trying to control someone with it, there's something more to the song, some hint of emotion that comes through. It's literally in our nature to imbue songs with our thoughts and emotions, and it takes years of hard work to be able to sing without letting anything through.

If you thought in the light of the sun, or let our hearts run free, if you gave your kisses gladly, if you could just let me be ...

Evidently my distraction allowed a little extra zing slip through into my voice, because I felt the man's attention, as if his gaze was a tangible thing.

The song, a bouncy ditty that Andrew had written by ripping off some long-dead poet, and which had about half the dragons present dancing, came to an end, and I lost sight of the man in the dazzle of the lights hitting us full on. I signaled to Andrew that I needed a break, and he gave Cassius the nod to swing into his ballad. I slipped behind the tower of speakers to get a sip of water, and gather my strength for what was to come.

I knelt there for a moment, contemplating running away, indulging in a brief daydream where I could escape, but the vibration of the stage beneath my knees seemed timed to a rhythm that spelled doom, doom, doom with every beat of the bass drum.

There was no escape, and I knew it. With a sigh of self-pity, I took one last sip of water and rose to my feet, waiting until Cassius had finished before moving forward to take my place at the microphone.

All three of my bandmates were watching me closely. Nervously, I wiped my palms on the flirty red dress that I wore at the gigs, and stepped forward.

Andrew gave me a few seconds, but when it was obvious I was just standing there all shades of awkwardness, he leaned forward into his mic and said, "We have a special song for you, one that you have to hear to believe. Ladies and gentlemen, Vicky ... er ... Montrose."

Mentally offering up an apology, I lowered my head, my eyes on the floor beneath my feet as I started to draw in the power that I needed to push. It flowed up through the ground to my shoes, up through my legs, and higher up to my torso, rising slowly up my throat, the tingle of it making me feel like I was standing in the middle of a lightning storm. I lifted my head, my mouth opening as I did so, and allowed the song to pour out of me. The words were meaningless, and in fact were never the same. They consisted of random bits of lyrics and poetry that stuck in my head, but what was important was the intention I put behind them. I pushed hard, compelling the people present to move their bodies to the beat of the music. Almost immediately they all started bobbing up and down in time.

Andrew waited a few seconds, then switched off most of the lights, leaving on only a few surrounding the stage in order to see. The sun had gone down a short while before, and shadows had long since claimed the grass, staining it black. The mass of bodies moved in time to the song, the music slowly dying away until there was just my voice.

Andrew moved away from his keyboard, gesturing toward the house. I nodded, and kept my push going, feeling it better to overdo it, since I had no idea how much energy it took to get dragons to comply.

Rina and Cassius followed Andrew toward the house, the last pocketing a pepper spray device that he would use to disable anyone outside my range.

I sang on, glancing at my watch, knowing I had to pace myself, but afraid to lighten up on the push. At the three-minute mark, I noticed something odd.

I was being stalked.

While the rest of the dragons danced, their bodies moving not in sync, but still together, one figure slid through them, slowly moving forward.

It was the man with the white stripe of hair. The panther man. And his eyes were on mine as he maneuvered his way through the dancing crowd, his gaze fixed on me.

Helpless to move while I was pouring energy into the song, I watched with growing horror as he started up the four steps to the stage.

He stopped in front of me, his face now perfectly visible in the sidelights. He had a long, straight nose, light brownish–dark blond hair that was swept back from the brow, and a square chin with a slight dimple that was barely hidden by light brown stubble. He had gray eyes that seemed to hold mine with an ease that made me even more uncomfortable, but there was something about those eyes ... something that was ... *more*. It was hard to put into words, but was as if time itself was etched into his eyes, leaving them with an expression that made me think of the stars slowly moving through the sky.

Holy hell, he's a handsome devil, was the first thought that went through my mind. The next was who was he, and what on earth was I going to do? I couldn't stop pushing the dragons lest the lure of my voice wasn't enough to keep them unaware of what the band was doing in the house, but it was clear this man wasn't in the slightest bit affected by me.

He just looked at me for a minute while I continued singing, then slowly walked around me, examining me from toes to nose, all the while I was trapped where I stood.

The man came to a stop in front of me, and said just one word. "Siren?"

Unable to help myself, I nodded.

"Ah," he said, then turned to look speculatively at the house before returning his gaze to me. "You would steal from my children?"

I opened my eyes even wider, although I hadn't thought that possible. His children? He couldn't be—

"No," the man said to himself, shaking his head. "Not children. Brothers. You steal from my kin."

There I was, bug-eyed, mouth opened as I sang some barely remembered Elizabethan sonnet, pushing the dragons before me into thinking they were having a truly excellent time dancing to some kick-ass techno music, and a foot away stood my doom.

Doom, doom, doom.

For a moment, I lost control of the push, and about a third of the dragons stopped dancing, but with a pleading glance at the handsome man with the compelling eyes, I sang on, spreading the push outward. The dragons all fell into line and danced again.

Except the man in front of me.

"You understand that I cannot allow this to happen," the man told me, his eyes so bright, it was like they were made up of mercury.

Desperately, I tried to split my focus and will him away, but I knew even before trying that would not work. For some reason, this man was immune to me, a truly horrifying thought.

"I will deal with you as soon as I stop your cohorts," he said, then turned on his heel and strode off into the night.

Panicking, I shifted the push from dancing to sleeping. I knew that wouldn't last for long, but it should buy me enough time to get the band out of the house, and make our escape before the big, bad dragons woke up and found out they'd been robbed.

Just who the hell was that man? He didn't look like a dragon, so he couldn't be that demigod that Andrew was so interested in … could he?

I sang a few more words, pushing sleep hard, and had the satisfaction of seeing the dancers slowly drop to their collective knees before toppling gently over to the side. There were one or two holdouts, but an extra push dropped them and the demon dog Jim.

"Now, just stay there!" I muttered as I leaped down off the stage and raced for the house. Halfway there, the sounds of crashing could be heard, followed by shouts and a couple of screams.

"Dammit, they're beating him up," I swore, pausing long enough to kick off my heels so I could run faster. I didn't even notice the gravel when I dashed across it to the stone of a verandah, flinging myself through an opened French door, and directly onto a warm wall that reeled back a step when I hit it.

"Hoorf," I gasped, my breath having been knocked out of me. Two hands came up to steady me when I rebounded off the wall, which turned out to be the man immune to my particular charms. There was a faint hint of a smile around his eyes and mouth, but it took me a minute before I could get air back into my lungs enough to say, "Are you all right?"

The look of amusement deepened. "Oddly, I was about to ask you the same thing. Do you need to sit down? You are bright red."

"Just the exertion of running to keep the band from hurting you." I looked around the room. It was dimly lit, but clearly empty. "Where … uh … did you happen to see … um …"

"Your friends are in the hallway." The expression in his lovely silver-gray eyes hardened. "They did not succeed in your plan."

"It was not *my* plan," I said quickly without thinking, then scooted backward until his hands fell from my arms. I edged around him and headed for the interior door.

He was at the door before I could blink, his back to it, his arms crossed, a slight frown pulling down two chocolate brown eyebrows. I swear his eyes were darker than they had been a moment ago. "It matters not who originated the plan. You cannot deny that you deliberately bespelled my chi—my dragonkin in order to steal from them."

I thought of denying it, but I've never been a good liar, and besides, he'd seen me in action. So instead, I crossed my own arms, and stepped up until I was a scant inch away from him. "I have no intention of denying it. Your dragonkin are rich. They can afford to lose a little without too much discomfort."

"That point is moot. Dragons do not take kindly to being robbed, no matter how many riches they possess." He leaned forward slightly so that his arms brushed against mine. An odd little jolt of awareness made me suddenly feel very hot. "We guard what is ours. You would do well to remember that, songbird."

I lifted my chin. I hate it when people try to intimidate me. "I'm a siren, not a bird. And I wasn't trying to take anything from your precious dragons … although you don't look like a dragon. Aren't you supposed to have weird eyes?"

His eyebrows rose a fraction. "Weird?"

"You know … elongated pupils, kind of catlike. Only you don't have that."

He blinked and suddenly, his pupils were long vertical stripes in his eyes.

"Holy shit!" Instinctively, I bolted, running through the door into a hallway, where I stumbled and almost fell over one of the three bodies lying prone on the floor. "Oh my god, you killed them!"

The dragon man was at my side, fortunately with his pupils back to normal, perfectly round black circles swimming in a sea of silver. "They are not dead. They are sleeping."

"What did you do to them?" I asked, stooping to check the pulse of the nearest person, who just happened to be Rina.

He shrugged. "I am the First Dragon."

"What's that supposed to mean?" I asked, and shook off the hand he put on my arm.

"It means I am the First Dragon."

"Let go of me."

"Why?"

"Because after seeing this, goddess knows what you'll do to me," I snapped, gesturing at my three unconscious bandmates.

He took hold of my arm again, and not being one to stand being manhandled, I punched him in the chest. "Let go!"

"I wish to escort you out to my kin. I do not think you will go unless I assist you," he said, and looked down to where my fist was still against his chest.

It was a very nice chest. Or at least, the part that I could see through his crisp white shirt was nice.

"Wait, First Dragon like … like Aisling mentioned? You're the god?"

"Demigod, as my son's mate would be the first to mention."

I cleared my throat and, gathering unto me every last bit of energy I could pull from the surroundings, walloped him with a compulsion that would have dropped a horse.

He didn't budge. He simply lifted one eyebrow and said in a mildly interested voice, "You wish me to do something? Ah, leave the house. That is my plan, as well. Let us go."

"Dammit! That was my best push," I said as he took me by my elbow and steered me toward the French doors. "Just my luck to get a god."

"I wasn't aware you had me," he said, pausing when we got to the edge of the verandah. He glanced down at my bare feet and, without another word, swung me up in his arms and carried me across the stretch of gravel.

"Hey! Oh. Thank you. I … uh … ditched my shoes because I thought the guys were beating … uh …" I didn't want to go on. I'd already made a big enough fool of myself. Besides, I had bigger worries. I had to get the band out of that house and into the van before the other dragons came out of my push.

"Because you thought I was being harmed?" He deposited me where I'd kicked off my shoes, which I hastily put on. "That is very noble of you, but it does not negate the fact that you attempted to steal from dragonkin."

"Look, Mr.—er—First Dragon …" I stopped, unable to keep from asking, "What is your name?"

He just looked at me with those gorgeous eyes. After about ten seconds, he answered, "First Dragon."

"Yeah, I know, that's what you are, but what's your name?"

"First Dragon," he repeated.

"You don't have a real name?"

"It is a name. It is what I am called. I am the First Dragon."

I gawked at him a minute, then asked, "You had a mother, right?"

"Most beings do, even demigods," he agreed, and with a hand on my lower back, gave me a gentle push toward the part of the garden where the dragons still slept.

"Right. So what did she call you?"

He said nothing for a few moments, clearly thinking. "Ah. I see what you are after. Yes, she had a different name for me."

I waited, but he just kept the pressure on my back so that I was moving forward.

"And that name was?"

He shot me a curious look. "Why do you wish to know?"

"Because, silly me, I like to know who I'm talking to. And yes, I know, you're the First Dragon, but that's what you are, not who you are, if you get me."

"Hmm." He seemed to think about that while he hustled me toward the side garden. "That is an interesting statement. I am not sure that it is true, but I am willing to discuss it with you at a later time. Regretfully, I see your spell has not yet broken."

We emerged from the hedge opening to find the garden full of prone bodies. I will admit to taking a moment of pride at the fact that the push had held so many dragons for so long, but that pride soon fizzled.

The First Dragon (dammit, what *was* his name?) surveyed the sleeping dragons for a few seconds, then suddenly clapped his hands together, the resulting sound making me stagger to the side a couple of steps.

"Criminy," I said, rubbing at my ears, which were ringing from the noise. Before us, the people began to stir, slowly sitting up and getting to their feet with murmurs of confusion. "You could have warned me before you did that."

The dragon slid me a look before turning to the dragons gathered. "You have been asleep, victim to a group of thieves. This woman bespelled you. Her companions are in the hall, bound and awaiting your justice."

"Oh, no," I groaned, trying to pull away my arm when the First Dragon took me by it and marched me forward.

"This woman is a siren."

"What is—Jim, dammit, get out of my way, I almost tripped over you." Aisling stumbled forward, steadied almost immediately by a tall man with black hair and the greenest eyes I'd ever seen. "What is a siren, exactly? Why were we on the ground? What was that noise? What in Pete's name happened? Oh, wait a sec, let me check in with the nanny."

Aisling pulled a small walkie-talkie out of her pocket and moved off a few feet, speaking into it.

"Told you she didn't smell right," Jim said, shaking itself so that black hair and slobber flew everywhere.

The First Dragon had been having a little chat with a couple of the men, and all of them suddenly turned and headed for the house, leaving me stranded in a sea of dragons who were becoming increasingly annoyed.

"A siren?" The dark-haired woman named May frowned. "Isn't that the women who lured sailors onto rocks so they'd drown?"

"Sirens are from Greek mythology," a boy of about thirteen or fourteen said, pushing his way through the dragons to consider me with soft brown eyes. His scrutiny was so impassionate, I felt a bit like a bug pinned to a board. "I read about them last year. They lured men to their death by making them wreck their ships."

"We don't do that anymore," I said indignantly, all the while trying to back up surreptitiously. The band needed my help, and I had a feeling the people before me weren't going to take kindly to my role. "That's so eighteenth century. Or so the only other siren I've ever met said, and she should know. She was an old lady then. She's probably dead now."

I was lying, but if there was one thing I'd discovered since finding out what I was, it was that you didn't rat out your fellow sirens. Not that I'd met more than the one.

I backed up a couple more steps.

"You put us to sleep?" Aisling asked, returning to the fold. She was frowning, and I began to think of a way to escape. I hated to leave the band behind, but this caper was their idea, not mine, and I was sure they would think nothing about sacrificing me for a chance at escape. "How? Did you use a glamour? I didn't feel one. Ysolde, you're the expert with magic—did you feel a glamour?"

A slight woman with long blond hair emerged. She was as tall as the teen, who continued to examine me just like I was some sort of curiosity, and shook her head. "I didn't feel anything other than the fact that Baltic and I had a great time dancing."

"We had a wonderful time, too," Aisling said, and others around her murmured.

I took another step back.

"Which is odd, when you think about it," she continued, turning her frown to me. "Since Drake hates dancing in public."

"You wouldn't know that the way you guys tango all around the house while you're wearing skimpy outfits," Jim said, giving Aisling a wink. "The last time he dipped you, I thought your boobs were going to pop out of that low-cut dress."

Her cheeks pinkened a little. "I said *in public*. Dancing in one's own home is perfectly normal. And the next time the Latin urge hits Drake, you are to look away, and yes, that's an order."

I took two steps back.

"Aw, man, you know how to take the fun out of spying," the demon said before turning to me. "Hey, she's getting away!"

I turned and bolted, flinging behind me a compulsion for everyone to look at something in the opposite direction. It would distract them for only a second or two, but that might be long enough to escape around the house to the van.

As it turns out, it wasn't.

"Hrnff!" I grunted when, halfway around the side of the house and heading for the drive where the van was parked, I was tackled from behind. It felt like someone had thrown a piano at me, and when I crawled forward from underneath my attacker, I found May glaring at me from narrowed eyes, one hand holding firmly to the back of my dress. "Damn, girl. You could have just yelled stop."

May released me long enough for me to get to my feet, wipe the grass from my face, and brush the dirt off my front. "Do you really think you can get away? Some of the most powerful dragons in Europe are here, right now, at this house. Running away is just going to make them angrier than they already are, and I can assure you that they're pretty well at the top of the anger meter."

"Of course they are. It would be asking too much of fate for anything else," I said with a sigh, resigning myself to capture when Aisling and a handful of other people ran over to us. At Aisling's orders, two men grabbed my arms and frog-marched me toward the house.

"We got her," Jim announced, walking ahead of me into the house. The room I'd entered before was now full of people, all of whom were furious. "She tried to bolt, but man, May has a pair of legs on her. She had Vicky here spittin' worms in no time."

"I did not, at any point, have worms in my mouth," I told the demon, and tried to look as if I had done nothing wrong. It was particularly difficult given that Andrew, Cassius, and Rina were now seated on a long sofa, their hands tied behind their backs. All three looked like they wanted to murder someone, and I had a bad, bad feeling I knew who they blamed. "Hello. Glad to see you awake."

Rina snarled something in Russian that I was thankful I didn't understand. Andrew held my gaze with his for a few seconds, then looked away. Cassius started spouting abuse and profanity until the green-eyed dragon snapped an order.

"There's no need to find duct tape," I said wearily, then gave them all a weak smile. Before anyone knew what I was doing, I turned to Cassius and sang a couple of lines from a popular dance tune, giving him a push to be compliant.

It was as if I'd dropped a bomb in the room. Andrew and Rina leaped up and tried to run for the French doors.

"She's singing again!" Aisling yelled, clapping her hands over her ears, while at the same time the green-eyed dragon shouted, "The thieves are escaping. Gabriel, stop them!"

All of the dragons began yelling at once, running around like mad people, shouting orders and making demands to stop the thieves, to stop me, and, most of all, to not listen to my song. I stood now silent in the center of the madness, and looked across the room at the only person who wasn't moving.

One side of his mouth quirked up for a moment. It was an annoyingly smug gesture but, at the same time, tugged at something inside of me. I couldn't help it—I gave him a little smile in return.

And then I was thrown into a room in the basement, and told to behave myself, or else the consequences would be dire.

I slumped against the rough cement wall, uncaring that I was going to make my pretty red dress filthy with decades of dust. "Great. This is just how I planned this day to end—alone, in a basement, with a house full of powerful immortals all calling for my head on a platter."

"Could be worse," a muffled voice said. I turned to see a shadow in the middle of the light at the bottom edge of the door. A heavy snuffling sound followed. "You could be in the mortal jail where your buddies are. Drake called the cops on them, and they just hauled them off. So count your blessings, babe. You still have us!"

I slumped all the way to the floor. Doom, doom, doom.

CHAPTER FOUR

"What are *you* doing here?"

The First Dragon closed the door of the room in which the siren was being held captive, and turned to evaluate her environment. Although perfectly clean, the chamber was clearly used as a storage facility, as it was partially filled with wooden packing crates. A small metal-frame bed had been placed in a corner, along with a round table and an uncomfortable-looking chair.

The last was occupied by the siren, whose face bore a fierce scowl.

"You aren't here to let me go, are you?" she continued, crossing her arms over her chest in a way that allowed him to fully appreciate the curves contained therein.

"Why would I do that?" he asked. "You tried to steal from my kin."

Her shoulders twitched. "I didn't steal anything. I just sang a couple of songs."

"Which allowed your friends to steal."

"Yeah, well, they aren't my friends." She looked away, studying the crate nearest her. "I just work with them. And before you get all judgmental, no, I do not consider helping thieves as my career. It's just something I have to do."

"Why?" he asked, seating himself on the corner of the small bed. It was highly uncomfortable.

She eyed him with distrust. "You want to know my life story? You? A demigod?"

"So far as I know, there is nothing that says I cannot be interested in the lives of mortals."

Her shoulders twitched again. "Where do you want me to start?"

"Wherever you feel your story begins."

Her lips curled in a delightful smile. He felt an answering smile on his own lips, and for a moment, he reveled in the emotion. It had been a long time since he had shared a simple joy with anyone.

"You really are different from other men, you know that?" She tipped her head to the side and gave him a visual once-over. "You don't say anything I expect you to say. You want my story? OK, I'll give it to you short and sweet: my parents dumped me as soon as they realized I wasn't normal. I spent some time in the foster system, running away pretty frequently because the families I got were horrible. I lived for a few weeks at a zoo, hiding in the buildings and eating the stashes of snacks the workers left. Then I ended up finally at the home of a woman who knew what I was. She was kind of Wiccan-lite, and knew that sirens were more or less outlawed in the Otherworld."

"That must have been a difficult life for a young girl," he said, admiring her strength in triumphing over such trials. He contemplated telling her that, but decided that now was not the moment. She was clearly not a person who was free with her trust, and he wanted to hear more of her experiences.

"It wasn't easy, that's for sure." She made a face and wiggled in the seat. "This chair is awful. My left butt cheek has gone numb."

He rose. "You may sit here."

"No, I wouldn't wish this chair on my worst enemy." She waved him back and then, after a moment's hesitation, sat on the bed, not close enough that she was touching him, but he felt the pull of her presence nonetheless.

What was happening? Was he so long out of the company of females that he was drawn to the first one he'd seen? But no, that could not be. He'd met some of the female dragons who were present for the party, and although he'd been mildly interested by them, it was the same interest he felt for all his children.

This woman was not his kin, and yet she held his interest like no one had since Maerwyn.

"I stayed with her—the last foster mom—until I was eighteen. Then I was officially kicked out of the system and had to go to work. I floated around for ten years doing odd jobs, and hiding from anyone who knew what I was."

He frowned. What had happened to the world that women such as her were considered dangerous? Could they not see the purity of her soul shining like a halo around her?

"Then I ran into Andrew—he's the leader of the band—and he recognized right away what I was, and they asked me to join. At first, it was just so they could throw some harmless glamours on the crowd, like making them want to dance, or feel happy, or even think the band was top-notch. But then he had the brilliant idea of me holding them in a thrall while they stole their valuables."

"Ah," he said. "And how did you react to that?"

She smacked him on his arm. "How do you think I reacted? I am not a thief! I told them I wasn't going to help them steal anything."

"They blackmailed you?" he asked.

"Yes." She slumped back, making him want to take her in his arms and comfort her.

And perhaps do a few other things.

"Andrew said if I didn't help them, he'd turn me in to the nearest Otherworld policeman, and claim I glamoured them into taking me into the band. The bastard."

"That is one word for it. I have others," he said.

She flashed a grin at him for a few seconds. He felt as if he were standing in the noonday sun. "I do, too, actually, but that's the most polite. That was two years ago, so now here I am, almost thirty, and I'm on the run with a gang of outlaws." She sighed, and asked, "How old are you?"

He was surprised by the question. "Why?"

A little blush pinkened her cheeks. "Just curious."

"I am old. I am the First Dragon."

"Yeah, we've been over that. But you were born, right? When was that?"

He thought. "I don't believe anyone kept track of the years then."

"What does that mean? Like Roman times?"

"No, I can remember the Romans spreading across many kingdoms."

"OK, we'll go a bit back. Ancient Egypt. The guys with the pyramids and those pharaohs who married their sisters, and all that."

"Before that. One of my brothers is a lord of their underworld."

"Wow, really? That's kind of mind-blowing. So much so that I think we're going to move on." Her brow wrinkled in thought. "What came before that? Um. OK, Iron Age."

He shook his head.

Her eyes widened. "Bronze Age? Stone?"

"The Stone Age people had excellent storytelling skills."

"Holy time lord. Do you remember people evolving from apes?"

"No. That is before my time." He smiled at her, marveling a little at how much he enjoyed talking to her. Perhaps finding another mate wasn't such a bad idea. But what would the siren think of such a thing?

"I'm trying, and I have to admit failing, to wrap my brain around just how old you are."

"Why does it matter?"

"I guess it really doesn't," she said after a moment's silence. "It's just ... well ... it's kind of nice to know you have something in common with someone you like being with."

He watched her cheeks flame, and wondered at that. "Why are you embarrassed?"

"Me? Who says I am?"

"You are blushing."

Her chin lifted in an obstinate gesture that secretly delighted him. "I just basically told you that I like you. That's kind of embarrassing considering we met a little more than an hour ago."

"Why?" he asked again, genuinely puzzled.

"Are you yanking my chain?" she asked, a flash of anger giving her voice a sharp edge.

"I don't believe so," he said carefully. "Assuming that is a colloquialism."

She gave a martyred sigh. "It is. Surely, even someone as old and out of it as you are can understand how ... awkward ... it is to admit you like someone when you just met them."

"Out if it," he murmured, turning the phrase over in his mind. Was he out of it? He didn't feel particularly unaware of modern life, but given what the siren had told him, perhaps he was. What he needed was someone to guide him through the intricacies of this current world. "I don't see why it is awkward. Would it help you if I said that I enjoy your presence?"

"I don't know if that helps or not," she said, her lips twitching as if she was fighting a smile. "But I appreciate that."

"Good." He sat, enjoying the silence and her nearness. He'd forgotten just how comforting it was to have a woman next to him.

"Well, this has been a delightful interlude, but I think it's about ended. Are you going to get me out of here, or not?" she asked, giving him a look that he felt down to his soul.

He made the decision at that moment.

"Yes," he said, and, without another word, left

the room. The red-haired guard stationed outside immediately locked the door after him.

"Hey!" he heard the siren yell after him. "Hey ... goddamn it, what is your name? ... come back here and let me out. Do you hear me? Let me out!"

Her voice followed him up the stairs to the main room, where the dragons were discussing the situation.

The First Dragon never expected to find himself so interested in the dealings of his children. To be sure, it was fascinating to see how the race had evolved since he had first claimed a mate and fathered the firstborn, but this—this was absorbing on a whole new level.

"We're going to have to call the Watch," Drake, the wyvern of the green dragons, said, striding past where the First Dragon claimed a chair. "We can't let her go, obviously, since god knows what she'll do to us in revenge."

"She didn't seem to me like a revenge sort of person," Aisling said, on her way out to answer a call from the nursery. "Don't do anything until I get back. Oh, hi, Ysolde. Yes, they're all in there. Baby duty calls."

"I just did that, myself. Anduin was out of bed and running around naked on the hunt for your twins. I had to ask your housekeeper to keep her eye on him. The little devil is the best escape artist. ..." Ysolde hurried in, giving the First Dragon a side-eye before seating herself next to her mate, Baltic. The First Dragon considered Baltic, his only living first-generation child. In many ways, Baltic took after him, preferring to be on the fringes whenever dragons gathered in a group, holding himself aloof, and watching rather than acting. But he also bore his mother's passion and sense of rightness, and it was both of those that had so touched the First Dragon's heart. Even now, Baltic's posture was studiously casual, but his eyes gave away the warmth of his love when he gazed upon his mate.

"That means getting Dr. Kostich involved," Gabriel said, glancing toward his mate, May. The First Dragon liked her—Gabriel called her his little bird, a name that fit her—but he knew little about the silver dragons. Born of a split with the black sept, they were the youngest of all his children ... with the exception of the reborn red dragons. Idly, he wondered how they were doing, and made a note to drop in and see for himself, once the period of the wager was over. "Kostich is going to be the only one who would have the power to take Vicky in. Unless we gag her somehow."

"Ugh," Ysolde said, frowning. "Surely that's not necessary."

"Vicky?" the First Dragon heard himself say, somewhat to his surprise. He hadn't intended on speaking.

"That's the siren," May explained.

"No, it is not," he corrected her.

May looked confused, and glanced at her mate for help.

"Do you know something, sir?" Gabriel asked.

The First Dragon decided he liked the silver wyvern. He was respectful, and clearly cherished his mate above all else. A romantic at heart, the First Dragon liked to see dragons appreciate their mates. "I know that her name is *not* Vicky."

The dragons present eyed one another before Drake asked, "If you have information about the siren, we would ask that you tell us."

"I do not know her name other than to say it is not Vicky. That name does not resonate with her. She must bear another."

"I see. Well …" Drake cast a glance at the others in the room. "You understand that the situation is a difficult one. The thieves were mortal, and although they clearly knew about members of the Otherworld, they are not part of it. The woman, whatever her name, is a different matter."

"Perhaps the First Dragon does not know about the interdict the Committee of the L'au-dela has placed upon sirens," Gabriel said.

"He knows," Baltic said. "As is he fond of pointing out, he's a god. There is little he does not know."

The other wyverns looked mildly uncomfortable. The First Dragon eyed his son, telling himself that he shouldn't encourage such disrespect, but it was ever thus with Baltic.

A memory suddenly returned to him of centuries past, when Baltic had taken his first steps, his tiny pudgy hands holding tight to the First Dragon's fingers, lurching forward with infinite glee at his newly discovered mobility. He remembered the joy in Maerwyn's face, how she applauded and praised the babe, and the swell of pride in his chest at the sight of them together.

A familiar ache of things lost returned him to the present. Absently, he rubbed a spot on his chest, and recalled himself to the conversation. He turned to Gabriel. "On the contrary, about this I am in ignorance. What is the L'au-dela?"

"The governing body of the Otherworld," Gabriel answered. "We dragons, through the weyr, have a treaty with the L'au-dela, so while we are not bound by their rules, in general, we live by them."

"It makes our lives easier," Drake agreed, moving over to a sofa when his mate returned to the room with murmured apologies. "On the whole. There have been some conflicts between them and Baltic."

"Words that I'm sure surprise no one in this room," the First Dragon said softly, with a little twist of his lips.

Baltic looked outraged, but Ysolde and Aisling both laughed.

"You talking about Kostich and the Committee?" Aisling asked. "He's bad news, even though he can be decent at times. Ysolde is our ambassador with the L'au-dela, Mr. First Dragon, and he gives her endless grief, but she's kind of used to that."

"I will admit that there are days when I'd dearly love to turn Dr. Kostich into a banana," Ysolde said, studiously buffing a fingernail against the material of her dress. "But for the most part, he's pretty by the book. If there is a law, he abides by it."

"And one of those laws is that sirens are absolutely forbidden to sing," Gabriel said, nodding. "Their magic is too powerful, with only a few beings who can resist them. That's why Dr. Kostich laid the interdict on them. There was one who ran around Europe a few decades ago, creating a disturbance in both the mortal and immortal worlds, but he had her confined."

The First Dragon frowned. He did not like the idea of someone confining the siren he had met. There was too much life in her, too much humor in her eyes, to be shut away from contact with others. Hadn't she suffered enough?

"They're pretty rare, though, aren't they?" May asked her mate. "I've never heard of a living siren, and Cyrene keeps me up-to-date with all the latest in elemental-being news."

"Cyrene?" the First Dragon asked, feeling momentarily out of his depth. It was unpleasant, almost as unpleasant as the feeling in his torso, the strange sensation of needing something. Not to mention his face itched. He rubbed a hand over his chin, and was startled to find whiskers.

"My twin," May explained. "She's a naiad."

"There's really no other option but to call Dr. Kostich," Drake said, reluctantly pulling a mobile phone from his pocket.

"Oh, sweetie, that seems so harsh," Aisling protested. "I liked Vicky … er … whatever her name is. Yes, I know her bandmates were trying to break into your lair, but that thing is practically nuclear-attack-proof, and we both know they wouldn't have gotten in there. It's not like Vicky … whoever … tried to break in, herself."

"She was the distraction to keep us busy while they attempted to do so," Drake answered, his eyes flashing a warning.

Aisling evidently wasn't intimidated. The First Dragon was secretly amused by this.

"Yes, but maybe she had a reason for doing it. Like how May was forced to steal stuff for Magoth," Aisling answered, gesturing toward May. "You know me—I'm a very good judge of character, and Vicky Whoever struck me as a very nice woman. There's got to be some reason she did what she did."

The look of momentary surprise that flickered across all the faces of the dragons present at Aisling's claim of character assessment did not escape the First Dragon, but no one disputed her. He agreed with her, however. The siren did not strike him as an immoral woman. The issue of her being blackmailed by her bandmates aside, she had come to save him from her friends.

"Maybe if we talked to her more," May said slowly. "We can find out if she's crafty."

The First Dragon lifted an eyebrow a fraction of an inch, just enough to tell May he knew what she was up to.

"Yeees," Ysolde drawled, giving him a considering look. "She looks like the type of person who might like nature, doesn't she?"

"Does she?" Aisling asked. "She didn't particularly strike me—oh! You mean, she's like … oh!" Aisling thought for a few seconds. "She's in a band, so she clearly likes parties. Wow. We did pretty good for just one day on the job, didn't we?"

"What did you do?" Drake demanded to know.

"It can't be this easy, can it?" May asked.

"I don't suppose it can. There has to be a drawback," Ysolde said, looking slightly disappointed.

The First Dragon felt an urge deep within that he hadn't felt in a long time—laughter was tickling him. How long had it been since he had laughed?

"What are you talking about?" Gabriel asked his mate.

"They're talking about a woman for him," Baltic said, nodding toward the First Dragon. "It's their wager. They think they've found her."

The urge to laugh grew within him. Trust Baltic to see the humor in the situation.

"The siren?" Drake looked flabbergasted.

"Why not? If she and the First Dragon hit it off, there's no reason—" Aisling stopped speaking when the door opened and one of Drake's two redheaded guards entered. "The prisoner is making a fuss," he said in a low tone.

"What sort of a fuss?" she asked. "Is she hurt?"

"No, she says she needs to use—" He gestured. "Facilities."

"She has to go potty? What's the big deal? Take her to a bathroom."

"She says she needs more than that." The man's face flared as red as his hair. He gestured toward his belly. "She says she needs ... things. And a shower."

"Things?" Aisling said, then enlightenment evidently dawning. "Oh, she needs ... gotcha. Well, you can bring her upstairs to one of the guest baths. She can take a shower there, and I'll give her whatever she needs."

Aisling started for the door, but Drake's "No! Not here!" stopped her in her tracks.

"Why not? I know you're all angry at her, and I'm not saying I don't feel a bit used, but it's against the woman code to turn down a woman in need of ... things ... and I'm certainly not going to make her sit there and be crampy and oozing and probably craving chocolate and potato chips, just to make a point."

The First Dragon filed away the question regarding chocolate and potato chips to ask the siren at a later date. He assumed she was having her woman's time, but did not see why Drake was forbidding the woman some comfort. He frowned at the green wyvern, letting him know he did not approve.

Drake looked taken aback at this gesture, but recovered quickly when Aisling, having said her piece, continued to the door. "You cannot bring her upstairs, *kincsem*. She is a danger, not just to us, but to the children."

"Oh, come on, now," May said, looking skeptical. "I'll admit that the whole gang is pretty unsavory, but I don't see them hurting children."

"You do not know the power of sirens," Gabriel told her. "I agree with Drake. The woman should not be allowed anywhere near people she can influence."

"We could gag her, I suppose," Drake said slowly.

"Like hell you will," Ysolde said, standing. The three mates were now standing together, facing the wyverns, their eyes bearing varying degrees of anger. The First Dragon enjoyed the scene immensely, and wondered if it would be appropriate to applaud the mates. "I agree with May and Aisling—Vicky, for lack of a better name, may be a victim in all this. Have you asked her? No, I thought not."

"Mate, you do not know—" Baltic started to say, but Ysolde rounded on him.

"Oh, I know. You, all three of you big strong dragons, you're all scared of one little woman, one you haven't even talked to, to find out just what she's doing here."

"We know what she's doing here," Drake said dryly. "She was robbing me blind."

"The rest of the band was," Ysolde insisted. "She wasn't even at the house."

"Actually, she was," the First Dragon found himself saying.

Everyone in the room turned to him. With slow grace, he rose to his feet, and rubbed his face again. He disliked this new sensation of whiskers, a side effect of having agreed to live as a modern dragon. That and the disagreeable feeling in his gut. He realized with a start that it was hunger, and immediately wondered if the siren was hungry, too.

"She was in the house, sir?" Gabriel asked. "You saw her?"

"Yes. She was trying to save me when she thought her companions were harming me. She is not, however, a thief. I have discussed it with her, and she explained how she came to be with them. It was not by her own choice." He turned to Aisling. "One of the needs you have bound upon me for a month is the desire to feed myself. You have food available?"

"You're ... you eat?" she asked, looking incredulous. She must have realized how rude that was, and immediately added, "I'm so sorry, I should have thought of that. Of course you're hungry—regular dragons get hungry, after all. We had dinner right before you got here, but I'm sure I can have something whipped up for you."

"And the siren," he said.

"Yes ... of course. She's probably hungry, too." Aisling glanced at Drake. "I'm sure Vicky won't cause any trouble while she's eating and bathing."

"No," Drake said, shaking his head. "Not in this house. Not with the children present."

"But—"

"The subject is not open to further discussion, Aisling." Drake was no longer standing alone—during the time he had spoken, the other two wyverns had moved in to flank him, just as the women tightened around Aisling.

The scene would have amused the First Dragon more, but the demand of his belly, and his desire to remove the siren from her imprisonment, preyed on his mind. Without addressing anyone in particular, he went to open the door, pausing to say, "The woman will dine and bathe with me."

All six people turned to look at him, identical expressions of astonishment on their faces. The First Dragon had no idea what had triggered that reaction, but he didn't particularly care. He had other concerns, one of which was to see the woman in more comfortable circumstances, while another was to feed his belly. And there was a pressure in his bladder that he remembered from his time living as a dragon with Maerwyn. He hoped his accommodations had a privy nearby.

"I ... you ... what?" Aisling finally stammered.

"She will remain with me in the gatehouse you have placed at my disposal. You said there were four bedchambers—she may have one. She will be confined to the domicile until such time as she decides what to do. You can have food sent to us?"

"Yes," Aisling said, blinking. "Certainly."

"What an excellent idea," Ysolde said smoothly, moving over to him and taking his arm. "The poor woman must be miserable in the cellar like that—I speak as a woman who suffers greatly at such times—

and it's the perfect solution because she won't be in this house at all, where she might sway people, and yet, will be held safe."

"And she'll be able to get to know the First Dragon," Aisling said with a bright smile. "And vice versa. Boy, this couldn't have worked out better if we arranged it!"

"But ... the First Dragon ... won't she simply sing at him?" May asked, following along with the others into the hall.

"I am immune, child of shadows."

"Oh, well, that's handy. ..."

The black demon dog emerged from a passageway. "Hey, Ash, the siren is down there bitching up a storm. You going to let her wash or not? Also, she requested a morphine drip, or at least a bottle of ibuprofen. Heya, Big Daddy. She had some pretty colorful things to say about you, also."

The First Dragon glanced at the demon, and set a ring of fire alight around its feet. He continued past in the direction the demon had come, ignoring the shouts of the dog.

"Sire of all dragons, I must caution you against taking the woman out from our control." Drake was on his heels, clearly not happy. "I am aware that her abilities have no power over you, but she has too much over the rest of the dragonkin, and I have little hope she would not use it at the first opportunity. You must know that above all else, we must protect what we hold, including those dear to us, and we cannot do that with such a threat loose."

"She will not be loose," the First Dragon told him, starting down the wooden stairs to the cellar. At the end, he could see Drake's bodyguard sitting on a chair with a book in hand. He rose hastily at the sight of the First Dragon, and stood awkwardly at attention at the door to the siren's chamber. "She will be under my guard."

"But you—" Drake stopped, evidently unable to find the words to continue.

"I'm having some things sent over to the guardhouse," Aisling called down the passage to them. "Ysolde and May went over to make sure everything is nice for you both. Jim, leave them alone. The First Dragon will fire you up again, and this time I won't put it out."

"I'm just helpin'," the dog told her, and nosed the First Dragon aside to bellow inside. "Help's on the way, babe! Tell your uterus to take a chill pill. Big Daddy is here to wash your back, too, heh heh heh."

The First Dragon leaned down to say softly, "Do you like being a dog?"

Jim glanced up, wary. "Yeah. Why?"

"I just wondered how you'd enjoy being a small dung beetle."

Jim's eyes widened, and it backed up, running immediately into Drake's legs. "Dude. It was just a joke."

"Not a very good one," the First Dragon said, straightening up.

"Big Daddy isn't going to wash your back after all," Jim bellowed at the door. "That was a joke. Tell him you don't like dung beetles, will ya?"

The First Dragon almost gave in to an eye roll.

There was silence from the cellar for a moment, and then the siren's voice drifted out to ask, "Why?"

"'Cause I think he's got the hots for you, and he'll listen to you." Jim flashed the First Dragon a cocky grin, but before the latter could do so much as set the demon's head on fire, it was off, tail whipping around the corner as the dog fled, leaving behind it, "Think I'll go help May and Soldy. Later taters!"

Drake sighed. "I would apologize to you for the demon, but I'm sure you are well aware that it has a favored status in our home. Aisling and the children are very fond of it, so I ask that you not destroy it."

"I wouldn't dream of doing so," the First Dragon said, and gestured toward the door.

The guard looked to his wyvern.

"We're taking the woman out." Drake answered the question in the guard's eyes with what the First Dragon felt was too judgmental a tone.

"But, you said—""The First Dragon has offered to be her captor, and of course, we must comply with his wishes."

"What's going on out there? Why is the blasted First Dragon not getting me out? He said he was!" The siren's voice was muffled, but perfectly audible.

Drake unlocked the door, and the woman staggered forward. The First Dragon caught her before she could fall, holding her hips while she regained her balance.

"You will go with the First Dragon," Drake told her.

"You will not use your voice around any dragons," Gabriel added, coming up behind them, clearly in the capacity of a guard.

Baltic sighed, and slowly followed suit. "You will not attempt to escape. Doing so will anger me."

The woman looked at Baltic. "And just *who* are you?"

"I am the dread wyvern Baltic," he answered, looking down his nose at her.

She looked utterly unimpressed, much to the First Dragon's amusement.

Baltic pointed at him. "I'm also one of the firstborn, a first-generation dragon. That is my father. Much though you might be tempted, as I have no doubt you will be, do not harm him."

She gave him a smile that was shy and yet warmed him to his toenails. "I wouldn't dream of it. Did Aisling mention ... er ..."

"She said you have your woman's time, and are uncomfortable," the First Dragon finished for her, and, taking her by the arm, led her toward the stairs. "You will have a bath at the house put at my use, after which you will dine with me. I feel a need for food, and you appear to me to be hungry."

"Really?" she said, her voice rich with amusement as he escorted her up the stairs, and through the hall to the double doors. "How on earth did you come by that deduction?"

"You are too thin. You don't eat enough," he told her, his fingers tightening slightly on her arm. "You need more flesh."

"Dear goddess, could you please clone yourself so that I can give one of you away to every woman in the world?"

He tucked away the word "clone" to be asked about later, not recognizing the term.

They reached the guesthouse, a pleasant building with two floors and a small walled garden. Beyond it stood the heavy black wrought iron gate that allowed visitors to pass onto the grounds.

"I'm going to want extra patrols guarding the fence and gate," he heard Drake say as they entered the house. "We'll have to use closed-circuit video to watch, since any of us would be vulnerable."

The First Dragon entered the small house absently musing on the fact that for the first time in several centuries, he was looking forward to having intercourse with a mortal.

Social intercourse, he mentally corrected himself, then indulged in another rare smile.

CHAPTER FIVE

I won't say that I didn't feel guilty when, as I was delivered to a bedroom in the gatehouse, I found May and Ysolde puttering around, unloading a stash of feminine hygiene products, body shampoos, and an assortment of garments.

I paused in the middle of the room, feeling all shades of awkward.

"Did you remember the chocolate?" Jim asked, pushing past me to nose around the garments laid out on the bed. "Aisling sent Istvan off to buy some salt and vinegar chips. She swears they work miracles for the men from Planet Abdo."

I stopped feeling guilty and stared at the demon dog. "The who from what?"

"You know, men from Planet Abdo. Abdomen. Get it? Heh heh."

"Ignore Jim," May said, giving the demon a tolerant look. "Its nose got out of joint with the arrival of baby Ava. We brought some of Aisling's clothes for you in case you didn't bring anything with you. And also some pads and tampons."

"We weren't sure which you preferred. I, myself, used to use a cup, but then I discovered this wonderful shot that takes care of everything," Ysolde said.

"Really?" Jim plopped its big butt down and looked interested. "They got a shot now? Will modern miracles of medicine never cease!"

"Out," Ysolde said, grabbing the dog by its collar, and hauling it to the door. "Go blight the First Dragon. Or better yet, go home."

"Gonna have some girl time, huh?" Jim said, nodding knowingly. "Can I stay if I'm quiet? 'Cause I've always wanted to hear what goes on in a dish session."

"No. Go away," said Ysolde.

"Aw, come on, Soldy. You know how I love to get in touch with my inner woman."

May gathered up an armload of feminine hygiene products and took them to the small attached bathroom.

"You going to talk about the divine feminine? Empowering your womb space? Dumping emotional sludge?"

"Jim, go away. Now, let's see. … Oh yes, I did bring some chocolate, but that's just because there's nothing that chocolate can't make better." Ysolde turned to a bag and pulled out a handful of candy bars. She grinned. "These are from Aisling's personal stash. There's both dark and milk chocolate."

"I know what's going on here," Jim said, wandering back into the room. "You're gonna talk about how to have vibrant orgasms, and that's why you don't want me around. But you're not thinking about the benefits I bring! Not only am I male, but I can take notes if you guys get too caught up in making Big O faces and stuff—"

Ysolde turned to the demon, shoved it out of the room, and set its tail on fire.

"Geez!" Jim said, promptly sitting down and doing a wiggle to extinguish the fire. "Some people just aren't open to sharing their experiences with others—"

Ysolde slammed the door closed in its face.

"I wasn't done talking!" Jim yelled through the door.

"We're done listening to you," Ysolde yelled back.

"But I got something to say to the Vickster."

I sighed, and opened the door. "What?"

It tipped its head and, I swear, winked at me. "It's kinda private."

"What?" I repeated, guilt making me sound more irritable than I was.

"I just thought you might want to know that you can't get it on with the First Dragon." The demon stood up, shook, checked its tail for signs of singeing, and sauntered down the hallway. I stared after it a minute, then hurried after it.

"What do you mean by that?" I stopped it at the top of the stairs. Drifting up from below, I could hear the rumble of masculine voices. No doubt the other dragons had come over with the First Dragon— dammit, I really would like to know his name—and were probably trying to convince him to turn me over to the Watch, the Otherworld's version of the police.

"Just what I said. The First Daddy can't get it on with mortals. Well, I mean, he can, probably—I don't know for sure, but I'll ask if you'd like—but there's a thing with demigods. They can't fall for mortals without losing their status."

"You're kidding."

The demon shook its furry head. "It's a thing. It makes sense, if you think about it."

"How on earth does anything so contrived make sense?" I demanded to know. "It sounds like a convoluted plot device."

"Or it's a fundamental precept that explains the difference between demigods and mortals," Jim said with a knowing look in its eyes. "You ever wonder why they got to be demigods in the first place? Stuff had to set them apart from the mortal race, and there has to be repercussions if those lines are breached. Otherwise, we'd just have demigods everywhere running everything, because nothing was there to stop them."

"Oh. I guess that makes sense." I thought about that for a minute. "It keeps everyone to their own, I assume."

"Mostly. I mean, if you knew that you'd lose your god status if you fell for a mortal, it would kind of keep you from looking too closely at them, wouldn't it?"

"I suppose so, but it's really a moot point. I like the First Dragon—he's an intriguing man—but I'm not looking to … er … hook up."

"Uh-huh," Jim said, smiling. "You just keep telling yourself that."

I returned to the bedroom to find Ysolde on her cell phone. "No, you may not. I don't care if it was run over—I will not have you carting home a deceased weasel. Brom—can we have this discussion another time? I have to get Vicky settled, and then go calm down Baltic. He's with the First Dragon, and you know how cranky that makes him. Leave the weasel where it is, and go back to the house. And be sure to close the gate. Drake will have kittens if you leave it open again."

May emerged from a small attached bathroom. "I put everything in the bathroom, Vicky. ... Er ... would you mind me asking what your real name is?"

I blinked at her for a couple of seconds, my mind whirling, what with dead weasels and demigods who couldn't have sex with mortals, and me stuck with a bunch of dragons who were being remarkably kind, given the situation. It was almost as if they had an ulterior motive. I wondered what that could be. "Vicky?"

"Eh? Oh. Er ... what makes you think Vicky isn't my name?"

"The First Dragon says it's not."

I made a face, thought about denying it, and decided there was little use. "My name is actually Charity."

"Pretty name," she said.

I gave a little half shrug. "It was a description more than a name. My parents dumped me without any information when I was about a year old. The foster-kid people thought it was amusing to give me that name."

"I'm sorry," May said, clearly uncomfortable, which just made me feel guilty all over again. "Is that why you steal?"

"It's a long story, but I would like to point out that I don't actually steal anything."

"But, you're working with people who do." Oddly, there was no anger or even accusation in May's eyes. I was a bit surprised by that. "Is there a reason you're doing so? I'm sorry if I'm prying, but I'm just trying to determine if there was a reason other than material gain that you are working with the thieves."

Now I was *really* surprised. It was as if the women could see through to my soul. "Assuming you are refering to my past, and the fact that I'm basically persecuted by the Otherworld police force, then yes, there is a reason I am with the band."

"We thought it must be something like that. We'll want the whole story later, but for now, we'll let you be so you can take a shower. Painkillers are in the bathroom," Ysolde said, tucking her phone away. "Aisling said to let her know if you need something else, like a hot water bottle. She also wants to know if you like needlework."

"Needlework?" I repeated, confused.

"Embroidery in particular."

Both women watched me closely.

"Sure. It's very pretty," I said, hoping I was making the right answer.

Ysolde and May beamed at me.

"Such a good fit," Ysolde said cryptically. "Be sure to tell us if you need anything more."

"I'm fine," I said miserably. I hated lying to people. "Thank you for everything."

"Not a problem at all. You have no idea the good you are going to do—" She paused when a bellowed yell could be heard from downstairs. "And that's right on schedule."

"What is?" I asked, somewhat startled by the vehemence in the voices coming up the stairs.

"The First Dragon has annoyed Baltic. I'd better go save him before he says things he shouldn't. Good night, Charity. It's been … interesting … meeting you."

"Good night. Thank you."

May murmured a good-night, as well, and both women left, trotting down the stairs to where I could hear raised voices.

I closed the door, leaning against it for a minute before running over to the window and throwing it open.

"Damn." There was no way down but jumping, and I couldn't think of many things I wanted to do less than jump out of a second-story building, especially when the first story evidently had tall ceilings.

"Looks like I'm stuck. Great job, Charity, really sterling work." I checked the bathroom to make sure there wasn't a handy exit (there wasn't), then returned to the bed, where I sat and promptly ate two candy bars. "Now what am I going to do?"

I thought of trying to call Andrew, but my cell phone had been taken when I was shoved into the cellar, and wasn't returned to me. Besides, if they were caught in the act of stealing and now in police custody, there was nothing I could do for them. Like me, they were on their own.

I wandered aimlessly around the room for a little bit, then decided I might as well have the bath that I'd led everyone to believe I desperately needed in my attempt to escape my prison.

There was a large claw-foot tub that dominated most of the bathroom, the kind two or three people could fit in. I ran the water, and opened the windows to allow the summer breeze in, since the room was a bit stuffy. By the time I sank into the steaming hot water (scented with some of Aisling's jasmine bath salts), my mind was quickly chugging through all the possible outcomes of the situation.

"One," I said, sinking into the water with a sigh of happiness. Even though the day was warm, there was nothing like a hot bath to relax your muscles. The soles of my feet stung a little, but the pain quickly eased. "The dragons call the Watch, and they put me away somewhere. Clearly, I'm not going to let that happen. Two, I escape and assuming the band gets let out of jail, and we get out of Hungary and lay low for a bit. Three, I escape and the band doesn't get out of jail, in which case I'm on the run again. Alone. With more people than ever after me."

I didn't really like the sound of any of that, but particularly of the last one. I'd been on my own for so long, it had been nice to be part of a group, even if that group had been using me.

The truth was that it had been a long time since I'd had any contact with people. I missed that. I missed the interactions, and feeling like I had a connection to someone. That I *mattered* to someone. I hadn't had anyone since my last foster mom Maud had died twelve years before.

"Poor Maud. I'm sorry I put you through such hell. You did such a nice thing rescuing me when no one else wanted me. But you're gone, and I'm alone, and what am I going to do?" Using my toes, I pulled the plug on the tub and got to my feet, shivering a little when a breeze suddenly swirled around my wet skin. I stepped out of the tub and went over to the counter, where a towel was folded. "I suppose that what I'm going to have to do is sing my way out of here and then go to—ack!"

The First Dragon stood in the doorway, looking bemused and slightly startled. I snatched up the towel and held it protectively in front of me. *"Mille pardons,"* he said, and gestured toward the open window in the bedroom. "I thought that perhaps you had tried to climb down. I take it your bath has made you feel better?"

"Yes," I said, more awkward than I've ever felt, and not just because I was stark naked in front of a powerful demigod. "It … I'm … I wasn't actually … oh, goddess. This is just a mess."

He glanced over my shoulder. "Do you need assistance? Would you like me to call one of the female mates?"

"No, I don't need—" I waved a dismissive hand. "I don't need anyone. The mess isn't me, or rather, it is, but not in the way that you think. The truth is, I'm not having my period."

He just looked at me with those uncanny, brilliant eyes, eyes that in this light had a touch of icy blue in their silver depths.

"My woman's time," I said, using his phrase. "I'm not having it. I won't for several months. My birth control takes care of that. And yes, I'm sure you don't particularly care about what's going on in my downstairs, but everyone is being so nice and sympathetic, and bringing me chocolate and pads, and I feel like the biggest heel in the world."

His eyes narrowed slightly as he puzzled this out, his gaze going over my shoulder again. "You used the excuse of your woman's time to get out of the cellar?" he finally asked. "I told you I would have you released."

"Yes, but then you left, and there I was stuck in that place. I hate being closed in, and besides, it wasn't very nice down there."

To my surprise, a little smile curled up the corners of his lips. "That is very clever bringing the mates to your side."

"And now I feel worse for using them." For some reason, tears pricked behind my eyes. I had a feeling they were based in self-pity, but that didn't make me feel any better. "I just ... I was desperate, and it seemed like the only thing to do, and dammit, I am *not* crying."

He wiped away one tear with his thumb, his fingers cupping my chin. "Then your face is leaking."

I couldn't help it—I laughed at the deadpan delivery of his delivery. "What I meant is that I normally do not cry over little things, and I'm more than a little ashamed that I'm standing here right now, nearly naked, and bawling over something so silly."

"Remorse, I've heard, can have that effect." He put his hand on my shoulder, his fingers warm. "Why did you not seek help to escape the control the musicians held over you?"

"Help from who? The Watch just wanted to put me away so that I couldn't affect anyone. There were several very wealthy individuals who promised to protect me, but I knew better. Honestly, the band was the lesser of two evils, and in return for me helping them take money from people they swore could afford the loss, they promised to keep me hidden from the nasty people who intended to use my powers in ways that made me sick."

He nodded. "You made the best out of an impossible situation."

His fingers moved gently on my shoulder, and I was aware again of just how warm they were. Very warm. So warm, it felt like my skin was on fire under them, but it was a pleasant burn, one that seemed to sink down into my blood.

"Um," I said, distracted by from my pity party by the burn he was firing up inside of me. "You have your hand on my shoulder."

"Yes, I do," he agreed. His gaze flickered past my ear again.

"My naked shoulder." The words seemed to come from my mouth without awareness, but that was likely because my whole being was focused on the sensation of his fingers on my bare flesh.

He stiffened slightly. "Does it displease you?"

"No. That is ... well ... not really. But it's kind of ... forward."

"Is it?"

"I didn't ask you to put your hand on my shoulder. My *naked* shoulder."

"You didn't ask to put your hand on my chest earlier, but I didn't complain," he pointed out.

Instantly, I stared at that bit of skin that showed through his opened shirt. I swear my mouth started watering just looking at it. Without realizing what I was doing, I put my hand on the open triangle of flesh.

His skin felt as hot as the fire inside me.

"You see?" He smiled, and I had to lock my knees to keep them from buckling. "I do not object."

We stood there for a moment, him with his hand on my shoulder, me with mine on his upper chest, and I suddenly realized that the tension in the air had to be addressed.

"I'm not a fool, you know." I let my fingers stroke the dip in his collarbone. "I know what you're thinking."

"I very much doubt that you do," he said with a flash of humor in his eyes. They were definitely more blue than they had been earlier ... or maybe it was just the lights?

"You're thinking that we're alone in a house together, and we're both adults, and you're handsome as sin, and we've both already admitted that we like each other, so there's no reason why we shouldn't hook up. But that doesn't mean that's going to happen."

A little frown pulled his eyebrows together. I waited for the inevitable question.

"Hook up?"

"Sex." I lifted my chin, and hiked my towel up a smidgen higher. "I'm not going to have sex with you. So if that's what you're thinking, you can just stop. For one thing, I don't jump into bed with men I've just met, especially when they are gods. And for another, I ... er ..." I stopped. My brain seemed to have run out of reasons why I shouldn't jump his bones.

"Don't engage in casual sexual congress?" He looked thoughtful, his fingers now absently stroking my shoulder. "I've always felt that an understanding of a sexual partner was the preferred method. Luckily, I am fairly understanding."

"In what way?" I asked, suddenly breathless. My heart started pounding like crazy, and I knew, I knew with every ounce of my being, that he was going to kiss me, and it was going to be the best kiss I'd ever had.

"I understand *you*." His gaze seemed to pierce all the guards I'd put up to keep people away from my true inner self, the light from those bright gray-blue eyes chasing away all the shadows.

I leaned in a little, unable to keep from smiling at the sheer folly of my feelings. "I do not fall for men right off the bat," I said, my breath fanning across his lips. "So don't even go there."

"The very last thought in my mind is that of seducing you," he said just before his mouth closed on mine. His hand slid from my shoulder, down my naked back, and stopping at my waist, leaving a trail of fire behind. Or at least that's what it felt like. I slipped my hand under his shirt, and enjoyed the warm velvet-over-steel feel of his chest, soft little hairs tickling my fingers.

"Good. Just so we're on the same page. Absolutely no sex." Those were the words that came out of my mouth, but my mind and body had very different ideas. I pushed him backward, out of the doorway and in a direct path for the bed, all the while nibbling on his lips. He tolerated that for about six seconds, but when he bumped up against the bed, both of his hands slid lower to my derriere, his fingers digging in as he pulled me upward, his tongue twining around mine, my mind and body and soul filling with fire.

"You must tell me if the fire gets too hot," he murmured against my lips. I was too busy divesting him of his shirt to pay much attention to his words, pausing to stare with wonder at the tattoo starting at the bottom of his breastbone before moving down to his belly button, and then curving around his right side to his back.

"It's a dragon," I said, tracing the intricate indigo-black lines. They looked Celtic in origin, the head and neck of the dragon stretched upward, and the body twisting around to the side. "I guess that makes sense, but I never thought of a god having a tattoo. Does it go all the way ..." I moved around behind him. The tattoo continued around his back, the Celtic coiled body forming a beautifully intricate pattern that held symbols within its scales. I followed the curving path around to his left front side, where the tail coiled around and dipped down into his waistband. "That's utterly gorgeous. Where did you get it?"

He nipped my shoulder, his hands sliding around to the front, discarding the towel I still held clutched to my front. "One of Alexander of Macedon's men did it. He thought it fitting. Does this hurt?"

I shivered at the sensation of the heat he licked across one breast. "Goddess, no. Do it again. And then do the other one." My fingers dug into the muscles of his shoulders for a second while the heat shimmered across now-aching nipples, and sank deep into my core.

He frowned at my breast for a second, then took one of my hands, and traced a symbol onto my palm. The symbol burst into flame, and instinctively I snatched my hand back, adrenaline jolting through my body. It was then that I realized the flame was warm on my hand, but not burning, not in the sense of normal flames.

"What ... what did you do?" I asked, staring at the symbol. It was a complex circle, one of the symbols that had been repeated on the dragon tattoo.

"It is dragon fire." He watched me for a couple of seconds. Then a slow smile spread across his face. "You can embrace dragon fire."

"I don't know about embrace it," I said, touching it with my fingers. It felt like a warm liquid, one that seemed very responsive to my desires. I turned my hand and placed my palm on his belly, pressing the fire into his flesh. "It is interesting, though."

"I am quite pleased to hear you say that." He kissed me again, and suddenly, my body was bathed in fire, inside and out, and for a moment I panicked. Heat consumed me, boiling my blood and crawling along my flesh, pushing me to the point where I was going to explode in a supernova, but just before it became unbearable, suddenly it became *my* fire. It twisted through me, turning my psyche into one blazing inferno of desire and need and power. I poured the fire onto the man before me, my mouth nipping and teasing and tasting his all the while my hands were frantically unbuckling his belt and working his zipper.

It was as if the fire had pushed me past the point of sanity. I threw caution to the wind, deciding my previous rules about hopping into bed with the first demigod I met were foolish. The First Dragon's hands were everywhere at the same time I was desperately trying to get him out of his pants, until at last we fell onto the bed in a tangle of arms, legs, and fire. I sat up, finding myself straddling his thighs, his belly under my hands. I was panting, my heart racing, the air almost crackling with static electricity.

"Do you ... you're a god. Is there anything different about how you do this?" I asked, unable to keep from sliding my hands up his belly to his pectorals.

"Different? Like this, perhaps?" His eyes were now molten gold, but thankfully, the pupils were normal. I made a mental note to ask him about why his eye color changed, but immediately forgot it when he smiled, and suddenly, I sat astride a dragon. Beneath my thighs, translucent scales shimmered, the colors in them moving and shifting along the spectrum, never just one color, but all colors.

"Holy shit!" I screamed, and would have leaped off him if the dragon hadn't disappeared and the man returned, his flesh wonderfully familiar and normal. I slapped both hands on his chest. "Don't you ever do that again!"

"Never?" he asked, humor and heat and passion in his eyes. "It is one of my forms, just as this is."

"What you do in your own time is your own business, but I'm very much a human form sort of girl, so if you expect me to impale myself on this really outstanding example of a penis—hoobah, that's really ... godlike ... isn't it? The word *heroic* comes to mind— then you are going to stay like you are right now."

He pulled me upward to claim my mouth again, an act that set me afire again. I wiggled against him, reveling in the feeling of his body beneath mine. He might be several centuries old, but he had the appearance of a man at the very peak of his physical prowess, and my body was singing its own siren songs to lure him into my depths. "It shall be as you desire."

"Good." I leaned down to lick the two little nipples

that hid in the soft brown hair of his chest. His hands were busy touching and teasing and stroking my breasts, leaving little trails of fire that absorbed into my skin, and drove my inner inferno even hotter. I paused to slant a glance upward at him. "There's just one thing."

His eyebrows rose in question.

"What we're doing is just a case of mutual itch scratching. There's nothing more at stake."

He stared at me for a moment as if he couldn't understand the words. I didn't want to come right out and tell him not to fall in love with me, because that was presumptuous to the nth degree, but at the same time, I didn't want to risk him losing his immortal state.

"Do you itch somewhere?" he finally asked.

"You know what I mean," I said, tapping my fingers on his chest.

"Yes," he agreed.

"Good. The second thing is that I can't make love to a man whose name I don't know. It's bad enough I'm jumping your bones a few hours after meeting you, but I'm putting that down to the fact that you're a god, and I haven't been with anyone in several years, and you're so incredibly hot that it makes my girl parts clamor for you. But I draw the line at doing it without knowing your name. I'll tell you mine first, since I dislike hypocrites: my name is Charity. Charity Doe, and yes, it's like Jane Doe. I don't know who my parents were. Now it's your turn, and please hurry, because my girl parts are screaming for me to stop talking and start with the action."

He smiled again, his eyes now more silver than gold, but still bright enough to almost glow with desire. He positioned me where he wanted me, my thighs astride his hips, and urged me down. My breath caught in my throat at the feeling of his intrusion into what were, by now, highly anticipatory parts, ones that welcomed him with tiny spasms of a million little muscles.

"My mother called me Avval," he said, his breath hot on my neck as he licked a path over to a spot behind my ear that made me weak. "It is Tajik for *first*."

"Fitting," I said, my body quivering around his as I worked out a rhythm that came close to making my eyes cross. His back arched beneath me, his fingers, which were now on my hips, digging in until they felt like claws. He breathed fire on me, bathing me in it, his body positioning into me, going to depths I hadn't known existed. And just as I trembled on the edge of an orgasm, he pushed me into it by suddenly twisting, flipping me over onto my back, my legs still gripping his hips. He said something in a language I didn't recognize, his voice hoarse, my entire being falling into an explosion of a thousand little pieces of ecstasy.

His mouth was hot on mine, kissing a path upward, his tongue lapping fire at a spot above my eyes before he suddenly relaxed on me, my brain too stunned by the power of the orgasm I'd just had to do more than desperately try to get some air into my lungs, and hope my heart wouldn't stop with the joy of it all.

"That ..." I was a bit surprised to hear a voice, then realized it was my own. I opened my eyes to find Avval draped across me, his breath steaming my neck. "That was the most spectacular orgasm of my life. Possibly that ever existed. If this is what it's like to be a god, then goddess above, you are the luckiest man on the face of the earth."

He lifted his head, shifting his body so that he was propped up on his elbows, his eyes now iceberg blue, but they were anything but cold. "I would agree with your statement, but you would likely misinterpret why, so instead, I will simply ask if you would sing for me."

I stared at him. "You want me to sing? But … why?"

He brushed a spot on my forehead. For a moment it stung. "Because I like music, and yours comes from your soul. Will it displease you to do so?"

"No. I …" I stopped for a moment, tears thickening painfully in my throat. "No one has ever asked me to sing for them. Oh, sure, plenty of people have wanted me to sing for their gain, in order to influence others, but no one has ever wanted me to truly just … sing."

He rolled off me, pulling me with him so that I was lying half across him. "I am not like the people you have met before. Sing for me."

I sang. And it was almost as good as the lovemaking we'd just shared, just as intimate, but satisfying on a whole different level.

It wasn't until I was drowsy and almost asleep that I remembered Jim's words about the fate of demigods who entangled themselves with mortals.

CHAPTER SIX

A horrible rumbling sound pulled the First Dragon from the edge of sleep. He lifted his head and looked down at his belly, unhappy with both the noise it was making and the hollow, needy sensation that accompanied it.

He was hungry. He disliked feeling hungry, and, in fact, felt somewhat helpless by it. In the days before when he had lived amongst the dragonkin, his mate fed him regularly. Maerwyn always saw to it that meals appeared just as his body was demanding sustenance, but now here he was, hungry.

He looked over at Charity. She slumbered beside him, her back to him, but her flesh pressed against his in a way that both comforted and aroused. How long had it been since he had taken a female? He thought, counting the centuries. Had it been so long since Maerwyn died? That sorrow seemed so ingrained in him that he had lost track of time.

He looked back at Charity, wondering what she would say if he asked her for food, but at that moment, he remembered the food that Aisling had promised to deliver. It was probably downstairs right at that moment, sitting there waiting to be eaten.

His stomach made the noise again. He grimaced and, propping himself up, leaned over Charity to murmur, "Food has been provided for us. Would you like to dine?"

"Mmm," she said, sleep heavy in her voice. She burrowed deeper into the pillow. "Had some chocolate already."

"I will eat," he said, and stroked a hand down her naked back, wondering again at the silken feeling of her flesh. He'd forgotten just how delightfully different females' bodies were from his, and he relished the sensation of reacquainting himself with all the intriguing nooks and crannies.

Charity made a purring noise, and wiggled into the blankets. He rose and tucked them carefully around her, pulling on his pants and shoes before making his way downstairs. The gatehouse had a small dining hall, a buttery, a solar, and two indoor privies. He made a quick visit to the last (reminding himself that dragons in the mortal plane had a lot to put up with), before going to find the food. He checked first the solar, but it was empty of food, as was the tiny dining hall. Finally, he entered the buttery—he checked himself even as he thought the word, and corrected it to the more modern word "kitchen"—where he found several packages of food that had been left.

This is a killer lasagna made with beef and lamb. Drake would eat a whole pan of it in one sitting if I'd let him, so I'm sure you and Not-Vicky will love it. Just peel off the plastic wrap and pop this in the microwave for ninety seconds to warm it up, read a note attached to one package. He pursed his lips, then said slowly, "Microwave." He wondered if Charity would mind if he woke her up and asked her to ready his food, but decided that if Maerwyn's reactions to such requests were anything to go by, Charity would likely mind it.

"I am the First Dragon," he told the container of food, and with a glance around that would have been called guilty in anyone else, he breathed fire on it.

Unfortunately, the container was of an inferior quality, and it melted along with the lasagna that the green wyvern loved so much. The First Dragon was mildly annoyed by that fact, and was torn between a walk to the main house to ask for more and the growing need in his belly. He left the mess of melted container and food where it was and turned to the other container.

Just in case Not-Vicky is a vegetarian, here is a green salad. There's a balsamic vinaigrette, and also a blue cheese dressing to go on it. Rolls are in the basket, and some pesto and smoked salmon are in the fridge. There's some ice cream in the freezer in case you get a sweet tooth. Just call if you need more food.

He poked into the bowl, and wrinkled his nose. It was full of greens. The feeling in his belly demanded more than greens. He looked around the rest of the buttery—kitchen—and discovered a basket full of crusty rolls, of which he immediately consumed four. Then he found a small dish of butter, which made the next three rolls go down much easier. He opened cupboard doors, discovering various plates and cups and assorted containers, but it wasn't until he opened a large cold cupboard that he found the other stores Aisling had mentioned.

He sat at the small table with his feast laid out before him.

"Pesto," he said, spreading some of it on a roll, "is quite satisfying. Also the salmon." He speared a piece of it and, after a moment's thought, put it onto the roll with the pesto, then topped it all with a tangy white sauce that he found in the cold cupboard. "Mayonnaise. It sounds French."

It took him some time to find something to drink, but he remembered a visit he'd made to his brother Osiris, and how Osiris had been insufferably smug about the running water he'd had installed at his palace in the Egyptian underworld. Sure enough, the gatehouse had a similar situation, and the First Dragon was able to quench the thirst that the consumption of twelve rolls had generated.

He took one last roll, put some pesto and salmon in it, and carefully carried it upstairs to present to Charity when she woke.

And that's when he discovered that she was gone.

He stared around the room in which he'd spent such a pleasurable time, unable to believe his eyes. "Charity?" He looked in the bathroom, where she'd stood so delightfully unaware that he could see her entire naked backside, but she wasn't in there. The bed was cool to the touch, indicating that she'd been gone for some time. Where had she gone? Had she returned to the main house, there to bespell his dragonkin?

He shook his head even as he thought it. She wouldn't do that. He knew her heart wasn't in the act she'd clearly been coerced into performing.

"She was abducted," he told the salmon and pesto roll, and then ate it while considering what to do. If he were not bound by a promise, he would simply slip into the Beyond, the plane of existence in which resided, amongst other beings, demigods. There, he would use the full scope of his powers and locate Charity. But he'd made an oath to his dragonkin, an oath that could not be broken. Therefore, he must act as a dragon would who was bound to the mortal plane. A minute later, he stood at the door to the main house.

"Wha—First Dragon!" The kin who opened the door was one of the green wyvern's personal guards. He had flaming red hair that was mussed as if he'd been roused from his bed, which, the First Dragon mused to himself as he entered the home, was likely what had happened. "You do us honor to grace the home of the green wyvern, of course, but … but is there something you need? Drake is asleep, as are all the wyverns and guests."

The First Dragon eyed him. "What name have you been given?"

"Pál, First Dragon," the guard said, bowing deeply. "It is my honor to be in service to Drake. And Aisling, of course."

"Of course." The First Dragon felt pleased with himself. Here he was, gripped in a sense of outrage and panic, and he made time to connect with one of his children. "Are you mated?"

An odd look passed over his face. "I … I have … she's not a dragon …"

"Ah. A mortal?"

Pal nodded.

"Thus are wyverns born," the First Dragon said, and, after a moment, patted the dragon's shoulder in a manner that implied that not all dragons were lucky enough to find a mate of the same species, but that he, the First Dragon, expressed admiration for the way that Pal bore up under that disadvantage. "The siren Charity has been stolen."

"She *what*?" Pal's voice rose on the last word.

"She was asleep, then she was gone. She would not have left of her own accord. Thus, someone must have stolen her away. Most likely the thieves who held her captive."

Pal blinked a couple of times, then pulled out what the First Dragon—who tried to stay current wherever possible—knew was a mobile phone. "My apologies for waking you, Drake, but the First Dragon is here. No, she's gone. Evidently really gone. The First Dragon believes she's been kidnapped by her band." He listened for a moment, then put the phone back in his pocket. "Drake will be down in a minute."

Almost immediately there was the sound of footsteps, and Drake clattered down the stairs, buttoning a shirt as he did so. He made an abrupt bow when he reached the bottom of the stairs, and asked, "When was she taken? Did you see the band members? How did they escape the mortal police?"

"I do not know. I was feeding my belly," the First Dragon answered. "Charity was upstairs sleeping when I left her, and when I returned with a roll for when she woke, I discovered she had been taken."

"When you left—" Abruptly Drake's teeth closed

on what he had been about to say. He ran a hand through his hair, then swore softly under his breath when Aisling hurried down the stairs, tying the belt of a dressing gown.

"What happened to Not-Vicky? Is she OK?" Aisling asked, stopping next to Drake. Behind them, the demon dog thundered down the stairs.

"Her name is Charity," the First Dragon told Aisling. "I do not know her status, but I have grave doubts that she went willingly."

"Why?" Aisling asked, brushing back her hair from her face.

Drake donned a martyred appearance. "The First Dragon was ... er ... with the siren before he went to eat the food you sent over."

"Yeah? So?" Aisling looked confused.

Jim sniggered and nudged Aisling's leg. "Told you he had the hots for her. Guess it pays to be a demigod, huh?"

Aisling's eyes widened. "You mean that you ... and she ... wow! That was even faster than I thought it would go, and I didn't even get a chance to give her an embroidery kit. I can't wait to tell the others. They'll be as delighted as I am."

Drake's look of martyrdom increased, but he pulled out a mobile phone and quickly made a call. "It's neither here nor there, nor any of our business. Bartholomew? Drake Vireo. I understand that Gabriel called you to take into custody the siren we found. It appears she's been kidnapped by her bandmates, who have somehow escaped the custody of the mortal police, and we'd like you to track—what? I see. Yes, quite fortuitous."

Drake's green eyes turned to the First Dragon, who suddenly found himself impatient. That in itself was annoying, since he did not, as a rule, feel such emotions, but now he had the distinct desire to snatch the mobile phone from Drake's hand and demand to know where Charity was.

"What's going on?" Aisling asked, trying to listen in to the phone. "Is that Savian? Tell him to stop by. Does he have Maura with him?"

Drake covered the phone with his hand, and said with a slight bow to the First Dragon, "It would appear that a thief taker that we called now has the siren. He found her hitchhiking into town, and recognized her from the pictures Gabriel texted."

"You called Savian after we told you not to?" Aisling looked furious.

Jim the demon whistled, and shook its head. "Dude. You know better than to cross one wyvern's mate, and you've got three of them under the same roof. Ain't nobody getting any nookie tonight. Well, except maybe Big Daddy."

Anger fired within the First Dragon, another rare emotion that he would prefer not experiencing. "Who is this thief taker?" he demanded to know.

"His name is Savian Bartholomew, and yes, Aisling, I know you and the other mates didn't want us to call him, but we cannot tolerate having someone so dangerous here. She has to be turned over to the Committee for protective custody."

"You'd think after living with her for so long that he'd have a clue, but it sure doesn't seem like it, huh?" Jim asked the First Dragon.

Fire blossomed at Drake's feet, and crawled up his legs. He gave his mate a long-suffering look. "Aisling, you are making a spectacle in front of the First Dragon. Control the fire."

"It's not of my doing," she snapped.

Drake looked aghast at the First Dragon.

He narrowed his eyes on the green wyvern. "I told you that Charity would be in my custody. No other was needed."

"Someone's up shit creek," Jim said sotto voce.

The green wyvern looked stricken, and stammered out, "We didn't think it right to impose such a burden on you."

"That is seriously annoying!" Aisling said, spinning on her heel and flipping her hair over her shoulder in the time-honored fashion of annoyed women before marching up the stairs. "I am so going to tattle on you to May and Ysolde."

"Aisling!" Smoke escaped Drake's nostrils as he gave his mate a potent glare.

She paused at the top of the stairs. "There are times when I wonder how you dragons survived all these centuries being so pigheaded," she snapped, and stormed off.

"I apologize for my mate's rudeness," Drake said, turning back to the First Dragon. "She has many excellent qualities, but control over her emotions is unfortunately not amongst them."

"Yeah, but you secretly love that, don'tcha?" Jim asked, giving Drake a wink.

"It is not your mate who needs to apologize," the First Dragon said, adding frustration to his list of unwelcome emotions. "I told you that I would be responsible for the confinement of Charity. For you to arrange to have her taken away by others is not acceptable."

"If I have in any way offended you, then I apologize. Naturally, we could not—oh, hell." Drake evidently remembered he had been on the mobile phone, for he put it back up to his ear. "Are you still there? No, I will not say hi to Jim for you, and you can accept Aisling's invitation another time. We have a situation here in that we've had a change of heart, and if you could just—that is not acceptable, no. We hired you to—I don't really give a damn about the L'au-dela, or what Dr. Kostich will do to your balls if you don't bring her to him. Just get the woman back here or—bloody hell."

"Uh-oh. Hung up on ya, did he?" Jim asked.

"Go help Aisling," Drake ordered the demon before squaring his shoulders and facing the First Dragon.

"You're not the boss of me," Jim replied, covertly wiping its slobbery lips on the back of Drake's leg. "Besides, she's in one of those moods where she really fills the demon lord bill."

"Then go blight someone else," Drake snarled, glaring at the demon.

"Yeah? Whatcha going to do if I don't—"

A green fire kindled in the wyvern's eyes.

"Fine, but if I miss any good bonking news, I'm going to tell Aisling you set me on fire again." The demon shuffled up the stairs after its master.

"I'm afraid the demon is correct about one thing," Drake said once it was gone. "The thief taker said he was en route to Dausen, where there is a portaling service.

From there, he will take a portal to Paris, where the siren will be turned over to Dr. Kostich, the archimage who runs the L'au-dela."

"An archimage." The First Dragon's lip twitched. He, himself, was a master of arcane magic, but it was not something that came naturally to his kin. "Charity would not like being with a man such as him."

"No one would like to be with him," the guard Pal said, then looked horrified that he'd spoken aloud.

"The thief taker must be stopped," the First Dragon decided. "Then we can rescue Charity from him. How long will it take to travel through the mortal plane to reach her?"

Drake was on his phone before the First Dragon finished speaking. "I'll bribe the portal shop owner to tell Savian the portal is down. That will force him to go into Budapest to find the only other shop in Hungary, which will give us time to track him down."

Drake moved off to hold a conversation with the portal owner.

The sense of frustration grew within the First Dragon. He disliked feeling helpless. It was foreign to him, and it wasn't something he intended on tolerating. "Do you have one of those machines?" he asked Pal.

"What machines?"

"The ones that transport you across the mortal plane."

"A car?" Pal glanced toward Drake, who was still on the phone. "Yes. Did you wish for me to drive you —
""Let us go find Charity," he said, and strode out the door. He felt better just taking action, although that soon faded when the act of getting the car and driving

after the thief taker ended up requiring not just Pal, but the other wyverns, and two of the mates.

"We should have taken two cars," Drake said, squishing himself into the backseat of the machine alongside the other two wyverns.

"I need no help, so long as your guard here manipulates the machine," the First Dragon said crisply. The idea that the others didn't realize he could rescue Charity on his own was annoying.

"After being responsible for the thief-taker capturing the siren? Aisling would kill me if I didn't help find her," Drake murmured, trying to make some space. "Gabriel, can you move over?"

Pal was at the steering mechanism of the machine, while the First Dragon sat beside him, the better, he thought to himself, to point out any tracks they saw that indicated the path the thief taker had followed.

"I'm pressed up closer to Baltic than I care to be as is," the silver wyvern answered.

"Then perhaps you should stay behind," Drake suggested.

"Oh, no, you're not going to leave me in the same doghouse you're in because we thought it best to have the siren removed. May made it quite clear that we need to resolve the situation. Baltic, this is not a time for manspreading! Do you mind not hogging *all* the seat?"

"My genitals require room. And I am crushed against the car door," Baltic answered, then grunted when Ysolde, who had crawled across the other two wyverns, sat down on his legs. "That is my spleen, mate."

"Eh. You don't need it. Sorry, May, let me just rearrange my legs."

"If there's no room, I can stay back with Aisling—" May started to say, but Gabriel reached across Drake, who was still trying to fit into the seat alongside the other two wyverns, and pulled her into the machine.

"And have you left out when Ysolde is here? No. Besides, you're the smallest of anyone."

"Perhaps if one of you would sit up with the First Dragon—" Baltic suggested.

The First Dragon settled back into the leather seat, and propped his elbows on the armrests. "I am quite comfortable."

"Got the door shut," Drake called from the back. "Go, Pal."

"What the hell do you have in your pocket, Drake?" Gabriel complained. "It's digging into my hip."

"Ow!" May turned to look over her shoulder at Ysolde.

"Sorry. I was trying to rearrange myself so I don't crush Baltic's noogies."

"Too late," came the reply from behind Ysolde.

"You have two sons," Drake said in a pained tone. "You don't need any more children."

"Says the man who has three," Baltic snapped.

"Two of them are twins! That's only two births—" May giggled. Ysolde started lecturing the wyverns to not fight until they reached their destination, which only made the wyverns argue more.

The First Dragon enjoyed the ride at the front of the machine, but he was worried, and he didn't quite know how to process the emotion. He wanted

Charity free from the thief taker, but what then? He couldn't very well confine her, for that put him in the role of gaoler, and he couldn't imagine embracing that situation. Nor would Charity appreciate it. No, he had to find a solution that would allow her to live her life as she desired.

He wondered if she missed him. He found himself missing her. He liked the way her eyes lit with humor. He liked the smell and feel of her. And most of all, he liked the way her presence filled the spaces around her.

He liked that she used the name his mother gave him. No one had done that since Maerwyn. No one had cared about his well-being since then, either. No one had sought to enjoy time spent with him once he was alone.

Not until he'd met Charity.

The dragonkin were right. It was time he took another mate.

He just hoped Charity saw it in the same light, and mused on that idea during the ride into town, where the portal stop was located.

"I will talk to the portal operator," Drake said as soon as the car came to a halt.

"You don't have to. I will," Baltic said immediately thereafter.

"I volunteer," Gabriel said, his voice muffled.

"I'll go," both May and Ysolde said at the same time, and to the First Dragon's surprise, the car more or less exploded with dragonkin. The doors popped open and dragons spilled out all over the pavement, a complicated tangle of arms and legs that was made more awkward by the fact that each dragon attempted to rise at the same time.

The First Dragon stepped over them and entered the portal shop, glancing around with interest at the furnishings. There were a number of cardboard boxes and wooden crates stacked along the walls. The counter was empty, but by the time the wyverns and their mates had pushed into the shop after the First Dragon, a slight, long-haired youth with a wispy goatee emerged from the back room, a half-eaten sandwich in one hand, and a rolled-up newspaper in the other.

"I called earlier," Drake said, pushing forward at the same time he straightened his shirt, and brushed back a lock of hair that had fallen forward. "About the thief taker Savian Bartholomew."

"Oh, right," the man said, nodding. "You're the dragon who promised big money to stop him. He was here about half an hour ago."

"You did not let him use the portal?" Drake asked, his brow darkening.

The man froze, then suddenly slammed the newspaper down on the counter. "Damned imps. They've gone invisible, which makes it a real bugger to catch them. What was that you said?"

Drake repeated his question with considerably more force.

"Naw, I told him what you said to say—that the portal was out of order, and that he'd have to use another one. It's not far from the truth—this portal is on its last legs, so to speak, and the shop is closing in the next couple of days. I'm going to Malta. No portals there. I'll make a fortune." He slammed the newspaper down again, this time triggering a slight "Eeek-eek" noise, followed by the scampering sound of a small invisible being.

"Excellent," Drake said, visibly relaxing and turning to the First Dragon. "It will take Bartholomew some two hours to get to Budapest. We can make some calls and have him picked up before he arrives.""He's not going to Budapest," the portal man said around a mouthful of sandwich. He sucked mustard off his fingers before realizing everyone was staring at him. "New portal shop opened up in Klas. Your friend's gone there."

Drake swore profanely. The First Dragon frowned at the portal man. "Where is this place?"

"About fifty kilometers to the west." The man squinted at a stack of books that perched on the edge of the counter, and slowly lifted his newspaper roll.

"Then we will go there," the First Dragon said, and quickly snatched out of apparently nothing the small imp that had been scampering unseen across the counter. He gave it a shake, and set it down on the floor. The *eek*ing that followed had a profoundly grateful tone.

"I don't think we should," Gabriel said, looking thoughtful. "We wouldn't get there in time to stop him."

The others agreed. "He's going to Paris. Is there any reason we can't take this portal and beat him there?" Ysolde asked.

The wyverns, to a man, groaned.

"Other than the fact that dragons don't portal well," Ysolde amended.

"What is difficult about a portal?" the First Dragon asked, giving a little frown at his children. Did they not see how important this was? Did they not understand that he had to save Charity? That he was obligated by a sense of duty? He had sworn to keep her under his protection, and he could not abandon that oath now.

"Dragonkin ... tend to get a bit ... *unsettled* by portals," Drake said slowly.

Gabriel rubbed his face and looked unhappy. "That's an understatement if I ever heard one."

"It's unpleasant as hell," Baltic agreed.

"Then you do not need to come with me," the First Dragon said with a bit of acid in his voice. Normally, he did not choose to let the dragonkin sense his unhappiness with them, but this was a desperate situation. He turned to the man who was still noisily chewing his food. "I will take the portal to Paris."

"OK. That'll be five hundred euros."

The First Dragon frowned. He had not dealt in a situation involving currency in many centuries.

Drake moved forward, the martyred look returning to his face while he pulled a wallet from his pocket. "We'll all take the portal to Paris."

"Christos," Baltic muttered, and added a few choice phrases, but stopped when Ysolde told him he could stay behind while the rest of them went off to save Charity.

"Just be aware that Cynthia—that's what I call the portal—Cynthia has been acting up a bit lately," the portal man said, leading the way to the portaling room after the payment had been made. "That's one reason why I'm closing her down. One or two people have reported the loss of minor body parts, but nothing important. Just keep your hands close to your torso."

The three wyverns stared at the portal with identical expressions of loathing.

"This should be fun!" May told Ysolde. "I haven't taken a portal in forever."

"Me either. Baltic always makes us fly places. I always did think it was kind of magical. One moment you're in one place, and poof! The next you're in another," she answered, taking off her shoes and tucking them under her arms.

"You'll forgive us if the next time you have a party, we send our regrets," Gabriel told Drake when the portal man flipped the switch that turned the power on to the large, swirling mass in the center of a stack of mattresses and pads. It hummed with energy.

Drake grimaced. "After what's happened at this one, I'm likely to miss the next, as well."

The First Dragon gave them all a stern look, then stepped into the twisting oval of light and matter and space and time.

CHAPTER SEVEN

"Aiieeeeeeecceee!" The word, more of a scream, really, came to an abrupt halt when I hit something soft, but solid. I shook my head, and pushed up, finding myself lying facedown on the sort of mats that gymnasts use, and looked around the room. I had an odd tickle in my nose like I was going to sneeze, but other than that, nothing seemed to be out of place. "So that's a portal. Wow."

A small brunette woman with a pink bow sitting on top of an elaborate 1960s hairstyle stepped forward, and said in a voice heavy with a French accent, "You must move, yes? There is another coming, and he will land upon you."

"Ack!" I leaped to my feet and spun around looking for the nearest exit. "That blasted thief taker Savian! I'll be damned if I let him hand me over to—" I stopped, hearing voices that sounded familiar in another room. I pointed at the wall. "What's in there?"

"The receiving *chambre*? It is where people go when they need to recover, you know?" She gave a Gallic shrug. "Not everyone, they have the power to portal *par excellence*."

The portal behind me started swirling even faster, warning me that Savian was coming. I debated running out of the building, but a familiar voice did amazing things to my insides, so instead I dashed for the door to the next room, slamming and locking the door behind me. When I turned to face the occupants, the sight that met my eyes was not at all what I was expecting.

The room contained two long olive green couches, and three bright orange overstuffed chairs. On the floor was a diamond-patterned rug. It also contained Drake Vireo, lying facedown, his hair standing on end, one sleeve of his shirt completely gone. At one of the couches, May was trying to get a completely naked Gabriel to sip from a cup of water. Like Drake, his hair stood on end, and he appeared to have two black eyes.

Ysolde was attempting to drag Baltic onto one of the chairs, but she'd managed to get only his torso onto it. He had one shoe on, and was wearing his tie around his head like a headband. He was also speaking in a way that sounded more garbled than an actual language. "I'm telling you that you need to sit up, and then I can find your other shoe. Stop trying to help, Baltic. Your legs aren't working right yet."

But it was the man propped up next to the wall that had me staring in surprise. Avval was sitting with his legs splayed out in front of him like a rag doll, his hair slicked back as if he'd wet it down, his hands twitching occasionally.

I hurried over to him, noting that Ysolde had given up on Baltic and was now checking on Drake.

"You came after me? That's so sweet of you. Kind of annoying, too, but really, I think the sweetness wins out. Are you OK?" I asked Avval, squatting next to him. "Did someone attack you? How did you know I was going to be here? Was it that annoying Savian? Are you, by any chance, rescuing me from him? Because if you are, I might cry."

His eyes were open, but they were unfocused. They were also ebony, with no difference between the pupil and the iris.

"Hrn," he said. "Fleng mit rnn."

"Dragons don't do portals well," May said, passing me with two paper cups of water in her hands. She gave me one. "They discombobulate them. Something to do with their molecular structure. Gabriel, do *not* get up, you haven't recovered yet. You'll just fa—there, see, I told you not to get up. Sorry, Drake. I hope he didn't hurt you."

She set down the water and helped Ysolde drag the naked Gabriel off Drake and back onto the couch.

I touched Avval's cheek. "Would you like a sip of water?"

"Flern," he told me, then made an effort to pull himself together, his arms and legs doing a brief swimming motion. "Charty."

"That's right, I'm Charity," I said soothingly, holding the cup to his lips. "Take a sip. Just one, I don't want you choking on it."

He put a hand up and managed to grasp mine as I let him have a few sips. "Found you."

"Yes, you did, that was very clever of you. Almost as clever as putting your clothes on backward."

He looked down, his eyes slowly focusing. His pants and shirt were indeed on backward. "That is... odd."

"It's the portal," Ysolde said, having rolled Drake over onto his back. He had blood on his lips, and was apparently missing a tooth. "Gabriel came out starkers, and Baltic is all out of sorts. Yes, yes, my love, I'll have someone find some dragon's blood. Just give me a moment to check Drake and talk to Charity, since it is her we came to find."

"Why?" I couldn't help but ask. "Why are you all here?"

"We couldn't let the First Dragon come all by himself. He doesn't know how to get around Paris, and besides, we all know what portals do to dragons," May said.

"Thank you. I think," I said, unsure of whether I was being rescued or recaptured.

"Just be thankful we didn't let Jim come with us," Ysolde said with a grimace.

"Why do you want to give them blood?" I asked, helping Avval when he tried to get to his feet. He was a bit wobbly, so I held on to his belt until he managed to stand up straight. "They don't look hurt."

"What? Oh, dragon's blood? It's a wine-based beverage, not actual blood," Ysolde said, *tsk*ing and taking the tie off Baltic's head. "Here, let me tidy you up and then you'll feel better."

"I'm going to see if the portal lady has any clothes handy, since Gabriel's appear to be lost to the portal—" May stopped, staring at Avval's back. "That's—the First Dragon has a dragon tattoo."

"Isn't it pretty?" His shirt was on backward, but not buttoned, so I pulled it off and helped him put his arms into it the proper way round. "The tail of it goes down his left thigh. ..." I paused as both May and Ysolde stared at me in openmouthed amazement.

I blushed what felt like five different shades of red.

Baltic pushed himself up off the chair, weaved heavily, then fell back onto it. "Knew it. He works fast when he wants to."

Avval, who was trying to reach behind himself to get at his fly, straightened up and gave Baltic a look that fathers had given sons for eons. "You forget yourself, Baltic. Apologize to Charity."

To my complete surprise, Baltic's expression turned contrite for about three seconds. "My apologies. I spoke without thinking. I blame the portal."

Avval snorted, but allowed me to move around behind him to unbuckle his belt.

"Um ..." I glanced at the other two ladies, then leaned in and whispered, "Are you wearing underwear? Because if you aren't, this is going to be a bit dicey."

He said nothing, just dropped his pants as soon as I unzipped them, and put them on the right way. I spent a few moments feeling smug because *my* dragon had all his garments, including undies, until I realized what my mind was doing.

The First Dragon was *not* mine. He was a demigod, one who could not get emotionally involved with a mortal being. Fun sexy times notwithstanding, he was nothing to me, and it had to remain that way no matter what my hopeful heart had been planning while I busy being kidnapped and stuffed through a portal against my will.

"What the everlasting hell is going on?" Another door that I hadn't noticed was thrown open, and the thief taker stood in the doorway, scowling first at me, then with growing astonishment at the dragons scattered around the room. "Holy hellballs. What did you do to them, siren?"

I opened my mouth to tell him, but I had no time to answer before he rushed forward, pulling a roll of duct tape from his pocket. He slapped a piece of tape over my mouth, and had me by one arm, pulling me toward the open door by the time I realized what had happened.

There was a roar of anger from behind me, and suddenly, Savian was pressed against the wall, held a good two feet off the ground by Avval.

A *furious* Avval. "What have you done, mortal?"

Savian squawked something, his face turning beet red. He clutched at the hand that held him by the throat, his legs kicking helplessly.

"Answer me!" Avval roared, and I swear the building shook.

I braced myself, then jerked off the tape, muttering under my breath and rubbing my abused lips while glaring at my erstwhile captor. "That's the second time today that you've done that, and I'm even less happy about it this time!"

"Savian!" May came into the room with a handful of clothing, having evidently caught the last part of the action. "You taped Charity's mouth shut? That's heinous!"

Savian made a gesture that would probably have been a shrug if he wasn't, at that moment, being throttled to death.

"I will not tolerate this," Avval thundered.

"You won't have to if you keep choking him like that," I said, tapping him gently on the hand that squeezed Savian's throat. "You might want to let him have some air so that he's still alive when I beat the ever-living tar out of him."

With a snarl, Avval released Savian, the latter falling to the ground with ragged, desperate gasps of air.

Avval spun around and demanded of Ysolde, "Release me from my oath so that I might smite this mortal."

"What? Me?" Ysolde, who had managed to get Baltic onto his feet, looked startled. Drake was also up on his feet, although he was clutching the back of a chair to keep upright.

"There will be no smiting on my behalf," I said calmly, although I managed to accidentally step on Savian's fingers.

He moaned and tried to crawl away, but Avval yanked him to his feet. "You will not take Charity to your overlord."

Savian, cradling his hand, said hoarsely, "My what, now? And just who are you?"

"Oh, do allow me to make the introductions. Savian, meet the First Dragon, the demigod who created the race of dragons. First Dragon, this is the man who picked me up on the way to the train station, slapped tape over my mouth so I couldn't sing, tied my hands behind my back, and dragged me over half the countryside of Hungary looking for a portal that worked." I glanced at my watch. It was almost dawn.

Avval looked as if I'd punched him in the balls. "You were not kidnapped by the musicians?"

"Not so much, no. I ... uh ... I thought it was best that I leave, and I didn't want to make a big deal about it."

"You left without telling me," Avval said, his eyes stricken. "Why did you not tell me so I could accompany you?"

The lack of sleep made me want to laugh at the outrage in his voice, but I knew he didn't see any humor in the situation. With a glance at the others, I took him by the arm and led him to the far corner. "I'm sorry I left without telling you."

"Why did you leave me?" There was pain in his eyes, now a bluish green.

I put a hand on his chest. The sensation of his warm chest under my fingers stirred all sorts of desires within me. "I didn't leave you so much as I escaped confinement. I woke up, and you weren't there, and it suddenly struck me that I was at the mercy of all the dragons, and you have to admit that you guys aren't particularly known for being merciful. I worried ..." I stopped, not wanting to admit the fright that had taken hold of me a few hours before and convinced me that I had to leave Avval.

"About what did you worry?"

I glanced at the others, but they were ignoring us to argue amongst themselves. It was on the tip of my tongue to say that I left because I didn't want to fall in love with him, since we could have no future together. Instead, I grabbed at the first excuse I could think of. "I worried that the other dragons would want to use me for their own gain."

"They would not," he said firmly, the pain easing from his eyes. "My kin hold what is theirs—that is true—but they do not resort to using another in order to gain those treasures."

"I'm sorry," I said contritely, relieved by the lecturing tone that had filled his voice. "That was thoughtless of me. The next time I escape, I'll take you with me, OK?"

He thought for a moment. "Very well. But do not forget your promise."

We returned to the others, only to be stopped by Savian.

"Wait a minute … demigod?" Savian squeaked, and looked shocked. "Did she say you are the First Dragon? *The* First Dragon? The one my Maura says has been seen only a handful of times in the last six centuries?

"Who's Maura?" I asked, not having a dragon player scorecard.

"My wife. She's a red dragon, or she was before she went rogue. Would you like to see a picture of her?"

Before I could tell him no, he whipped out his phone, and started flipping through a gallery of pictures. "There she is on the beach. This one is when we went to Disneyland. And here's Savian Jr. Maura says he looks like me, but I think he has her eyes. Maura's convinced he's going to be a wyvern someday. And here he is sitting up. Isn't that brilliant of him? Only seven months old and he's already sitting. Takes a superior sort of baby to sit up that early, let me tell you. I've got a photo somewhere of him dressed up for Mardi Gras. …"

"I can't believe you tied up Charity," May said, shaking her head. "Bad form, Savian."

"The only reason he took the bonds off was because the portal lady said they might kill me if I portaled with them on, and he didn't want to lose some bounty that was offered for me."

Drake made an odd choking cough, but studiously brushed off what remained of his shirt. May had gotten Gabriel into a pair of white cotton beachcomber pants, and a bright pink shirt dotted with lime green llamas.

I looked nobly martyred. "Goddess knows what would have happened if he hadn't heeded her warning."

"There's something you should know about that bounty," Ysolde said, giving her dragon a long look.

"Another time, perhaps," Gabriel said quickly, and the other two wyverns made noises of agreement, while Avval just made a low rumbling sound deep in his chest. "What we should be doing is making sure Charity is all right, and then planning what to do next."

"What you will do next is leave her alone." Avval took my hand and gazed at them all with eyes that were now a rich brown color with touches of red and gold. "She is not a possession to be passed around, nor is she a danger to anyone." The last was said quite pointedly to Savian.

"I relinquish my claim," Savian said wisely, giving the First Dragon a bow. "I know when I'm bested. Maura will be delighted when I tell her that I met you. I don't suppose we could do a quick selfie?"

The First Dragon stood as if made of stone while Savian leaned close and snapped a couple of pictures. Any other man would have edged out of the room quietly, but not my captor. He appeared to be oblivious to the waves of icy fury that rolled off Avval.

"So then everything is solved?" Ysolde asked, looking somewhat disappointed. "We found Charity, and Savian isn't taking her to Dr. Kostich, so everything is fine, right?"

"Everything is far from fine," I said, drooping a little from exhaustion.

"You are tired," Avval told me. "You must have rest. Also, my body now requires rest." He shot a little glare at Ysolde, who tried very hard to look innocent. "We will rest together, and then we will discuss what is to be done with this one who confined and abducted you."

"My wife is a dragon," Savian said, raising his hand. "My son could be a wyvern. You wouldn't want to do anything to leave them without a husband and father, would you?"

"There are ways to keep you alive and still make you suffer," the First Dragon said softly. "Leave now before I show you those ways."

Savian blanched. "There's … uh … there's just one problem."

"What is that?" Avval did not look like he wanted to keep talking to Savian. "Why are you still here? I have dismissed you."

"It's …" He slid me an apologetic look. "It's just that the Venediger keeps a pretty tight control on Paris."

I leaned toward Ysolde. "What's—""The Venediger runs the Otherworld side of Paris."

"Ah. Thanks."

Savian was explaining the same thing to the First Dragon. "Well, she runs most of Europe, really. And one of the things she does is monitor the portals."

Avval was impatience personified, and gestured sharply. "You speak words that make no sense. Either say what you mean or leave."

Savian looked faintly ill now. "It's Charity. There are alarms attached to the portal. When Charity came through it, the Venediger would have been notified that a siren was in town, and by law, she would have to report it to the Committee."

"Oh, great. So Dr. Kostich *does* know she's here?" Ysolde leaned against Baltic. "Now we're going to have to see him again, and he'll call you fat, and I'll have to practice magic at him, and you know that never ends well."

"We will discuss your role in this later," Avval said grimly to Savian. The latter slipped away with murmured apologies.

Avval turned to Baltic. "You have a domicile in this city?"

"No, but Drake does."

Drake, looking put-upon, murmured something about it being his honor to welcome the First Dragon— and everyone else—to his Paris house.

"We will go there, and rest," Avval announced, and gently pushed me toward the entrance.

"You know, by rights I should take off and not look back," I commented, waiting at the outer room while the other dragons gathered up their various items. "Just run away and not look back."

"Run away?" Avval looked suddenly interested. "You mean a chase?"

"No, I mean I'd run away from you. From all of you. That's basically what I did earlier tonight. Oy." I ran a hand through my hair. "I guess that was last night."

"We will discuss that situation in more detail at a later time," he replied with a long, completely unreadable look. "My stomach indicates it wants feeding again. I do not know how dragonkin get anything done with these constant demands by your body. My face itches, and I believe I will need to use the privy again soon. My bladder is almost as demanding as my belly."

"I'm sure Drake has food at his Paris house, and probably a dozen bathrooms. And yes, we can talk about what I did another time—I simply brought it up to say that I'm aware I should be running away from you, but that I'm not."

"I would be happy to chase you if you like," he said politely.

"Chase me? Chase me where?" I couldn't help but ask.

"If I told you where to run, then it would not be a true chase."

I wondered if I was more tired than I knew, or if Avval had suddenly decided he lived in Wonderland, and was going to talk in riddles. "I don't think I understand what you're talking about. Why do you want to chase me?"

"A chase?" Baltic and Ysolde entered the outer room, Drake on their heels. "You're having a chase? Ysolde!"

"Oooh, I haven't had a chase in forever."

"We're doing a chase?" May asked, and stopped abruptly in the doorway. She turned to yell into the room, "Gabriel, they're going to have a chase! Hurry up!"

"What in the name of all that is sleep-deprived is this hullabaloo about a chase?" I asked anyone who cared to answer.

May giggled. Ysolde smiled brightly. Drake swore under his breath.

"Dragons chase," Avval said simply. "It is pleasurable."

"How so?"

"Trust us, it's pleasurable," Ysolde said, with May nodding fervently in the background.

I looked through the glass windows out at the city. Paris had not yet woken up, the air still indigo, but with light fingers along the eastern sky. Absently, I slipped off my shoes and fingered the long strip of duct tape that Savian had used on my hands. Evidently, I'd shoved the tape into my pocket after he'd removed it.

What on earth was I doing? my inner siren asked. Why was I even there, allowing myself to be tempted by Avval's nearness, and thinking thoughts in which I had no right to indulge? *The man is a demigod,* I reminded myself. A being so far above me I couldn't even conceive of what his life was like.

I did know one thing—I liked him. *A lot.* And I wasn't going to be responsible for making him miserable by damning him to a mortal life.

"Well," I said, pushing open the door into the predawn Paris. "It's been a long day. Maybe another time we can … oh!"

I'd turned back while speaking, and now gasped and stared over the shoulders of all the dragons. They all turned to look back at what had so startled me. I shoved the door closed and, using the duct tape, wrapped it around the two vertical handles on the glass doors.

Avval was the first one to realize what I'd done. The expression on his face—surprise mingled with a hot flare of passion—remained with me as I bolted down the street, did a one-footed hopping seriocomic spin around the corner, and ran like mad into predawn Paris. Distantly, I could hear a roar, but didn't stop to examine why I acted as I did. I had made the right choice in Hungary when I slipped out of the house while Avval was eating, and I'd made it again now.

My life was not one I could share with anyone, even if he was willing to give up everything he loved for me. Not with what amounted to the whole of the Otherworld wanting to either imprison me or use me.

As I ran around another corner, a black car that had been traveling toward me suddenly slammed on its brakes. I glanced over my shoulder to see two men emerging from the car, both racing toward me. A third man, tall and imposing, emerged, and shouted orders to not let me get away.

"Bloody, bloody hell," I swore, and jetted down the street, dashing across the traffic without a mind to the honks and yells from the drivers who were out this early, and ran straight for a patch of green that I had glimpsed through the buildings.

Sounds of commotion followed while I flung myself around corners, ducked under awnings, and avoided both pedestrians and cars alike, my eyes fixed to the garden that was ahead. The black wrought iron fence around it meant I had to skid to a halt and look frantically up and down the street to find an entrance, wasting precious seconds. Behind me, voices shouted, car brakes squealed, more horns honked, and above it all, my heart pounded in my ears. I spotted an entrance about a block away, and raced for it, mindless of the pain of small pebbles grinding into my bare soles. I had just reached the entrance when I was suddenly thrown forward a good dozen feet, a white-blue flash of light dazzling me for a few seconds. For the second time in twenty-four hours, I found myself facedown on the ground, spitting out blades of grass.

CHAPTER EIGHT

Here's a pro tip for people who might be the subject of an arcane magic explosion: don't expect to be able to recover immediately from the effects of it. It took me a couple of minutes before my mind (and eyes—arcane magic is bright!) cleared, and I had my wits about me again. By that time, my hands were bound behind my back, and two large men in dark suits were hauling me to my feet. The third man, the one in authority, was striding toward us with an extremely annoyed expression. I shook my head and sagged against my captors, waiting for the third man to get closer. He started throwing around orders as soon as he could be heard.

"Gérard, gag the siren. Emile, have you bound her hands? She evidently had no difficulty escaping the thief taker, although that is not surprising since the man is an idiot who—"I lifted my head the second his foot touched the grass, and sang.

The man froze. The two men holding on to my arms dropped them and went still. I sang a popular song about relationships turned bad, and behind it, I put a massive push to put the three men into a catatonic state. The third man resisted a bit, but went under after a few extra pushes sent in his direction.

Behind him, Avval suddenly appeared, his lovely hair a bit mussed, his eyes glowing bright gold.

"Charity! Why are you singing?"

I gestured toward the man in front of me, and turned so he could cut my bonds.

He snapped them off with his bare hands (making my inner siren squeal with delight), and spun me around, his hands hard on my arms. "Do you know what the chase does to a dragon?"

I stopped singing, keeping an eye on the three men. "May and Ysolde said it was fun. I gather you get some sort of jollies over being a predator hunting prey?"

"It stirs the primal being in us. It makes the sophisticated dragon of today hark back to the early days when we struggled to rise above our baser natures, when it was a matter of fighting merely to survive. The need to possess was vital to our being, for without our power we would have been consumed by those who strove to eliminate us." His eyes were so bright, they almost hurt to look at, and for the first time, I felt—I truly felt—his dragon nature. This wasn't just a respected elder: this was a man who created a race of beings from nothing, forming and shaping them against forces that must have been overwhelming.

"You really are the *first* dragon," I said, touching his jaw, filled with admiration and awe and no little pride that I had known such a being.

"That is a long time in the past. As my children point out, there is life to be lived now." He lifted my hand to his mouth, his lips caressing my fingers in a way that made all my internal organs melt into puddles of happy goo.

Emotion swamped me then. Hope gave way to desire, and finally to something strange and wonderful, a painful aching that left me wanting to beg, "With me. Live your life with me!"

The words trembled on my lips just as I leaned in to kiss him.

"—couldn't find his arse with both hands. Why my granddaughter Maura married him is beyond my understanding." The man who gave orders suddenly came back to life, glancing around him in surprise. His eyes landed on first me, then Avval, sight of the latter causing him to take a step backward. "The dragon ancestor. Don't tell me Tully Sullivan has died again and you've come to resurrect her?"

Avval frowned at him. "I do not know who you are, or of whom you speak, but I suspect you are responsible for binding Charity's wrists. I do not take kindly to abuse of her."

"I am Dr. Kostich, head of the L'au-dela Committee."

"Ah. The archimage." Avval did an amazing thing then—he managed to give the impression of looking down his nose at Dr. Kostich without actually doing so. "Your interference is not welcome. You may leave."

Dr. Kostich was obviously a man who recognized just what a unique being Avval was, but just as obviously, he didn't like the fact that he more or less had to kowtow to him. After a few moments of visual struggle, he finally gestured toward me and said, "This woman poses a danger to the entire Otherworld. She cannot be allowed to run amok."

"Oh, you haven't seen me run amok," I said, annoyed as hell that he'd interrupted what was probably going to be a humdinger of a kiss. "You want to see it? Because I'm happy to do it. Watch me put the entire town to sleep!"

I took a deep breath, but Avval stopped me by sliding his arm around my waist, and pulling me up to his side. I stared at him in utter surprise.

"If you so fear her in your world, then she will simply reside elsewhere," he said calmly.

Dr. Kostich's gaze flickered back and forth between Avval and me. "I see. I ... yes, I believe I see."

"I'm glad you do, because I don't," I snapped, pushing myself away from Avval. "You're not talking about killing me, are you? Because you can't look at me one minute like you want me to take off all your clothes and touch you everywhere, and lick that fabulous tattoo from dragon head to pointy tail, and do all of the things that I suddenly can't stop thinking about, and in the next want to take me off this mortal coil."

"On the contrary," he said with a slow smile that set fire to my soul. Literally. Fire burst out at my feet and slowly climbed upward. "I intend to do just that."

I stared at him, confused, until he pulled me against him, his lips teasing mine, his fire burning bright in and around me when he said softly, "I do not abide in the mortal plane, Charity. You will come into the Beyond with me, and share your life with me. You will be away from the threats posed by ignorance and fear, and will sing for me whenever you like, not because you are trying to save yourself, but because you wish to."

"The Beyond? That's like another form of reality, isn't it?"

"Of a sort, yes. I have a home there, with gardens, and fountains, and animals of all sorts. Do you like animals?"

"So long as they don't bite or sting me, yes. What do you do in your house?"

"Whatever I desire."

I sighed a little, my heart yearning for what I knew it couldn't have—a home. One filled with security and love. "That sounds idyllic."

He was silent for a moment, his thumb stroking my cheek. "It was for a while. Of late, it has made me aware of just how alone I am. How separated from my kin I am. And how empty my home is."

Tears pricked my eyes when he bent down to kiss me, tears of gratitude mingled with heartbreaking sadness. He must have noticed, because he broke off the kiss to gaze at me with eyes that were turning a bronze color. "Why do you weep?"

"I can't stay with you," I said softly, wishing like hell that Dr. Kostich wasn't standing there listening to us.

To my surprise, he turned around and walked away, going to the entrance of the park before stopping. The two men who had captured me were still under the spell of my push, and mindlessly unaware of what was going on around them.

A little frown ruined Avval's smooth forehead. "This makes no sense."

"Unfortunately, it makes every sort of sense." I took a deep breath. I'd never before opened up my heart to anyone, man or woman, and doing so now made me feel incredibly vulnerable, but there was nothing for it. "If I stay with you, I'm going to fall madly in love with you. To be honest, I think I'm partly there now, since there's nothing I want more than to spend my days and nights with you, watching your eyes change, and listening to you talk about your dragonkin, and catching that little smile you make when you think no one is watching, and … oh, a hundred other things. But I can't."

"You have someone binding you here?" he asked, looking around as if such a person would suddenly manifest. "I did not sense a claim upon your heart, but perhaps living as a modern dragon has affected my ability to judge such things."

I put a hand on his chest, right over where his heart beat so strong and true beneath my fingers, the tears in my eyes calling my throat to ache. "No, there is no one here for me. But that's just the point—if I go with you, I'll fall wholly and completely in love with you, and then you'll love me back, and then we'll both be miserable because you won't be a god anymore, and you'll have to come back here and be a mortal, and then they'll capture me again, and we won't be together."

His frown deepened. "What is this? Why would I be mortal?"

"You know." I nudged him. "That rule where gods can't love mortals without losing their powers."

He stared at me as if I suddenly had a hundred Newfoundland dog demons dancing on my head.

"There is no such rule. I do not live by rules. I am as you see me. Nothing can change that."

"Jim told me you couldn't fall in love with me, because then you'd be mortal."

"He lied."

I gawked at him for the count of three, then swore. "That bastard! I bet he told me that whopper because he's a demon!"

"More likely that he thought telling you we had no future would make you want to have one with me." Avval's eyes were alight with humor.

"Regardless, when I see him again, I'm going to sing him into a pretzel shape that will take him a week to untangle."

Amusement smoothed his brow again, and lit his eyes with bright silver lights amongst the bronze. "You are so sure that I will love you in return? I am the First Dragon."

"You are that and much, much more, including a very sexy man who has a warm and loving heart, one that doesn't dally with women without having some sort of an emotional bond." I leaned close and whispered in his ear. "Just like you, I have a sense about these things, and you're falling in love with me, too. I see it in your eyes, I feel it in the way your lips touch mine, and I know it by the way your fire flows from you to me."

His mouth was hot in answer, his kiss everything I knew it would be—pushing me higher and higher until I was a blazing sun, burning bright in the glow of his love.

"Come with me," he said at last, when I could breathe (and think) again. "Be my mate. Live forever with me in the safety of the Beyond, and watch my dragonkin grow and flourish."

"Oh, yes," I said, suddenly limp with happiness. He laughed then, a rich sound, one that filled with me with infinite joy, and scooping me up, he swung me in a circle before taking my hand and kissing my palm.

"Ouch!" I snatched back my hand at the sudden burning sensation, staring in surprise at the dark brown mark. It reminded me of a diamond-shaped flower, one bearing four main blossoms, but with four small leaves between. "What on earth? Did you brand me?"

"You are my mate," he said with satisfaction. "All mates carry such a mark. Are you ready to leave the mortal plane now?"

"We can go now?" I asked, glancing around the park. The sun was coming up, and people were emerging from their homes to take to the street. "Right here? We don't have to go somewhere special?"

He reached out into the air, and made a gesture that left a complicated pattern of light in the air. "Anywhere I am with you is special."

I punched him in the arm. "Stop it. You're going to make me cry, and I'm already moist of eye because you said nice things to me, and you want me to be your mate, and you're offering me a haven. Are you sure, Avval? Are you really sure?"

He disappeared into the pattern of light flecks that danced on the air. For a moment, time froze, my brain stuttering to a stop at the realization that he had left me, just left me.

Then his hand emerged from the light, and his voice, that deep, infinitely smooth voice, reached out to me. "Come, mate. I will bring you home."

EPILOGUE

From: Ysolde (tsullivan@magenet.org)
To: Mates Union Members
Subject: Welcome to the newest mate!

Ladies, I'd like to introduce you all to Charity. She's gone and done the impossible—taken the First Dragon off our hands—and for that I'm infinitely grateful. Now Brom can sleep in peace without fearing the FD will pop in and try to turn him into a dragon. Now Baltic won't be subjected to visits wherein the FD stands around moodily and makes him (Baltic) feel guilty about everything. Now I won't have to put up with any more of his (FD's) cryptic remarks about me fulfilling the promise that he sees in my future, which, I swear, if I hear just once more, I'm going to shank someone.

Anyway, welcome Charity.

From: May (shadowalker@silverdragonsdoitbetter.com)
To: Mates Union Members
Subject: Woot!

I'm so glad you're one of us now, Charity. Hope your chase went well. Gabriel and I ended up in the Tuileries, where we were almost caught by a group of tourists.

From: Bea (Imcharming@constantineinc.com)
To: Mates Union Members
Subject: What???

The First Dragon has a mate? When did this go down?

From: Aisling (guardian5242@guardiansguild.org)
To: Mates Union Members
Subject: Charity

She met him here, Bea, at Ava's party. I wish you could have been here. Although in hindsight, it's probably better if Gary stayed away from crowds—I wouldn't want him getting stepped on. Jim sends its love, btw. It asked me to have you ask Constantine if Gary can come for a visit sometime.

From: Aoife (sonotcrazy@blackdragonmarket.co.uk)
To: Mates Union Members
Subject: I second the what!

I'm happy for the First Dragon, and of course, equally happy to have a new mate to hang with, but holy cheeseballs, people! Who knew the First D. could have a mate?

From: Sophea (sophea@dragonbreakers.org)
To: Mates Union Members
Subject: ???

So … I'm not the new kid on the block anymore? Yay for that. And welcome, Charity. I look forward to meeting you and seeing how His Royal Interferingness is doing (remind me to tell you how he has a habit of materializing just when things are getting hot and heavy with the dragon of your choice).

From: Aisling (guardian5242@guardiansguild.org)
To: Mates Union Members
Subject: Charity, part two

Not sure if she can actually see these e-mails in the Beyond. Maybe May can fill us in on that at our next meeting, which is next month on Tuesday the fourteenth, at our house in London. I hope you can all still make it. Drake says he wants the *sárkány* that got messed up because of the portal, and everyone having to fly home, and evidently you all had chases that took you all over Paris (which I'm insanely jealous about, because there's nothing I love more than a chase, but I know I'm preaching to the choir).

I do hope Charity can make it, but assuming she can't, because Dr. Kostich meant what he said when he swore he'd have her arrested if she comes back into our world, perhaps we can Skype with her. We'll have to see if the First Dragon has Wi-Fi.

See you all next month!

Aisling closed up the laptop, checked that Ava was snoozing soundly, and went to find the dragon of her dreams.

He was downstairs in his study, at his own laptop. "Are you finished?" he asked, rising when she entered the room.

"Yup. Mates Union business all finished."

"Did you ask Bea about Gary coming for a visit?" Jim asked from where it lay on the floor reading a gentlemen's magazine.

"Yes, I made the invitation, although don't get your hopes up. You know how fond of Constantine and Bea Gary is." She made a face. "Which, given that he's a disembodied head, is a bit odd, when you think about it, but meh. I'm just not going to think about it. Jim, stay."

"What?" The demon looked up, startled, then started snickering when Aisling pulled Drake toward the door. "Oh man, it's that time again, is it? You going to chase him, or have him chase you this time?"

"None of your business," Aisling said, and, blowing a kiss to the demon, left the room.

Drake waited until they were outside the house, the balmy evening air filled with calls from night birds. "We've had three chases already this week, *kincsem*. Are you sure you're up for another one?"

"You're not losing your taste for it, are you?" She leaned forward and kissed him, relishing the roar of fire that never failed to follow.

"I would have to be dead a good sixty years for that to happen," he answered, his green eyes glittering in the dark. "Would you like me to go inside to give you a head start, or—"He stopped, stiffening for a moment at the sound that drifted toward them.

"Oh," Aisling said on a breath, turning to face the same direction. "Someone's singing. Isn't that beautiful? It makes me want to cry, and dance, and shout with happiness at the same time. It's like a hundred songs all compressed down into one perfect bit of music. You don't think—"

Drake smiled, but it was a smile filled with heat, his attention wholly on her. "I think you had best run, *kincsem*. Run now, before Charity finishes her song."

Aisling ran, her heart filled with joy both at the dragon who was patiently counting to fifty so that she had a head start, and for the music that was lifting over the night, bringing happiness to everyone within its sound.

KEEP READING FOR A
DRAGON SEPT SHORT
STORY FEATURING
JIM THE DEMON DOG!

THE
PERILS OF
EFFRIJIM

CHAPTER ONE

"Now remember, this is a vacation, not carte blanche for you to run amok and be obnoxious."

I made a little pout, which let me tell you, ain't easy when your face is shaped like a Newfoundland dog's muzzle. Which mine was by dint of the fact that my most magnificent form to date was that of an extremely handsome, debonair, and utterly fabulous Newfie. "Have I ever run amok and been obnoxious?" I asked my demon lord, a kinda clueless Guardian by the name of Aisling Grey.

She lifted her hand and prepared to tick items off her fingers.

"Yeah, yeah, whatever," I interrupted before she could get going on what may or may not have been a few unfortunate incidents in my past. "Kiss kiss. Have a nice time on Drake's yacht. Don't let the door hit you on the ass on the way out."

"It's not too late to send it to the Akasha," Drake said as he walked past me, a baby carrier in each hand. "You would be able to enjoy our vacation without worrying about whether or not the demon was causing trouble."

"Hello! 'The demon,' as you so rudely referred to me, is standin' right here!" I gave Drake a look, but he missed it entirely. You'd think that a guy who just happened to be a wyvern, leader of a group of dragons who marched around the earth in human form, would be a little more aware of things, but Drake was like that, always missing my pithy comments and witty repartee. "And Aisling wouldn't send me to the Akasha. That's the cruelest thing a demon lord can do to her charming, adorable, and entirely innocent demon, one who, it might be pointed out, was recently praised for actions above and beyond the call of duty with regards to the birthing of the spawn."

Drake muttered something extremely rude in Hungarian under his breath as he took the spawns out to the car.

"One," Aisling said, doing that finger-ticking-off thing again. She made mean eyes at me as she did it. "You will cease referring to the twins as 'the spawn.' They have names; use them. Two, yes, you were of great assistance when it came to their birth, especially since you had to don human form to do so."

I made a face. "Man, that was totally sucky. You should have seen the size of my package in human form. It lacked, babe. It just lacked."

"Two and a half—you will not tell me, in any terms whatsoever, about your genitalia, be it in doggy or human form."

I rolled my eyes. "Sheesh, Ash, loosen up a bit. I didn't go into actual measurements or set up a website devoted to it."

"For which the world is truly grateful."

THE PERILS OF EFFRIJIM

"Yeah, well, I'm still peeved at May for making me take that form. Human form is just so boring."

"May was doing the best she could given a bad situation," Aisling said, pointing to a suitcase sitting near the door when István, one of Drake's elite guard, came in from where the car was waiting to take Aisling and Drake to a yacht he'd hired for a couple of week's vacation. "Just that one is left, István. Are you and Suzanne set for your trip to New York?"

"Yes, we will leave as soon as Jim is picked up."

"You make it sound like I have babysitter," I grumbled, a bit annoyed. "You know, I'm over a thousand years old—I think I can take care of myself for ten days. Just leave me a credit card and the number of the local pizza place, and I'll have a Mrs. Peel-athon while you're gone. And maybe a Morgan Fairchild-athon. Rawr."

"Now there's a recipe for disaster." Aisling's lips thinned as she continued. "Three: you will obey Anastasia. I have formally given her the right to give you orders, and you will respect that, and do as she commands."

"She just better not let that creepy apprentice of hers around me," I said, scratching an itchy spot behind my ear. "During that lunch you dragged me to meet Anastasia, that Margarine Chip chick looked like she wanted to gut me."

"Buttercup is Anastasia's apprentice, and unused to demons," she said, her nostrils flaring in that nostril-flaring way she had. "You will be polite and courteous to both of them, do you understand?"

"Yeah, yeah, keep my nose clean, gotcha," I said,

wandering over to my favorite British newspaper, the one with the girls flaunting their bare boobies. "So long as Anastasia takes me to Paris to be with my darling Cecile, we're all good."

"Four: while you are visiting Cecile, you will do anything that Amelie asks you, and you will leave when Anastasia says it's time to leave. You are not to beg Amelie to stay with Cecile. She is a Welsh Corgi. She can survive the nights without you. "

"I don't see why I have to spend the nights at a hotel with Anastasia," I said, tapping my toes on the picture of a particularly busty chick. "It would be easier for everyone if she just dumped me off at Amelie's and let me have my vacation there, with Cecile, rather than picking me up every night like it was some sort of day care or something."

"Five," Aisling said as Drake reappeared at the door, giving her a raised eyebrow. "You will remember that if you step out of line, the Akasha awaits."

"You wouldn't really let anyone send me there," I said, rubbing my head on her leg just to let her know I'd miss her. "There's no way out of the Akasha unless you're summoned out, or get a special dispensation from the Sovereign. You don't know 'cause you've never been there, but it's hell, Aisling, it's really hell. Worse, 'cause Abaddon ain't that bad once you figure out how to avoid the torture seminars. But the Akasha? Brrr. Bad mojo all around."

"Just you remember that when Anastasia gets here. Are you all packed?"

I nodded toward the doggy backpack she got me for the visits I made to Paris to hang out with

my lovely Cecile, she of the tailless butt, and oh, so
suckable ears. Corgies may be low to the ground, but
they are the sexiest things on four legs, and my Cecile
was particularly snuffleworthy, even if she did get a bit
grumpy now and then. "Eh? What?" I realized suddenly
Aisling had been droning on about something or other.

"Kincsem, we will be late for the train if you do
not leave now," Drake said, taking her by the arms and
steering her toward the door.

"I asked you if you have your cell phone and the
phone book with the emergency numbers in your
backpack."

"Yup, all there. And extra drool bibs, that nice
bamboo brush, a clean collar, and a two-week supply
of Welsh Corgi Fanciers for when Cecile is napping."

Drake rolled his eyes and pushed Aisling through
the door over her protests.

"Be good!" she bellowed as he shoved her into the
car.

"Don't forget to bring me back a present!" I yelled
back, and waved goodbye before slamming shut the
door and heading straight for Drake's library and the
leather couch they always forbade me to sit on.

That's where Suzanne found me almost an hour
later. "Your substitute Guardian is here," she said,
frowning. "Did Aisling say you could sit on Drake's
nice sofa?"

"What Drake doesn't know can't cheese him off,"
I said, sauntering out, waiting patiently while Suzanne
fetched my backpack.

"Hiya babe," I said, greeting the white-haired
Guardian Aisling's mentor Nora had dug up to

accompany me on my trip to Paris. Anastasia wasn't really my idea of a babe, her being approximately a million years old (or at least looking like it), but I'm nothing if not Mr. Smooth Moves, and I know how the ladies like a little flattery. I did a quick gender check on her (nose to crotch, just to be polite), then sucked in my gut while Suzanne strapped on the backpack.

"Good afternoon, Effrijim," Anastasia said, smiling vaguely. I was pleased to see that her weirdo apprentice wasn't around. "Are you ready to fly to Paris?"

"Been ready all day," I said, accompanying her to the door. She said goodbye to Suzanne, who waved at me (I gave her hand a quick lick goodbye), and waited for me to go first. "I'm glad to see your uber creepy assistant isn't here. She really freaks me out, you know? I think she has something against demons in incredibly handsome doggy form ...oh, hi Butterball."

"My name is Buttercup!" The woman who stood waiting at the limo that Drake had arranged for us (against his will, but Aisling has him wrapped all around her fingers), narrowed her beady little eyes at me. "Can we not just banish the demon, mistress?"

I snickered, about to make a comment about BDSM, but Anastasia's gentle, elderly voice stopped me. She was a nice old lady, so I didn't feel right about shocking her with references to stuff like bondage.

"Aisling has assured me that Effrijim will be on its very best behavior, and I'm quite sure that it will be so," she said, giving me a kind of vague smile as she got into the limo.

"Absotively," I agreed, shouldering the buttery one aside so I could sit next to Anastasia. "Hey, do you mind if we stop at a McDonald's on the way to the airport? I didn't have much lunch and I'm famished."

"But mistress—" Buttercup started to protest, but it did no good. I flashed her a charming grin before settling back in the seat.

"No, my dear. I know the demon offends you, but consider this a good learning experience. Aisling claims it is harmless and after meeting it, I am in complete agreement." She flashed a smile my way. "Effrijim is too much of a gentleman to cause trouble, I'm quite sure."

I straightened up a little, pleased by the gentleman comment. "Damn straight. Although ya know, you can just call me Jim rather than Effrijim. I really don't use it much 'cause it's kinda sissy sounding, don't you think?"

"Not at all. I think it's quite distinguished. It suits you," she said nicely. I rubbed my face on her just because she didn't think the name was awful (it is, but she didn't admit that, which wins beaucoup brownie points in my book). "I must admit that I'm a bit curious as to why you chose to adopt the form of a dog when you could have appeared in human form."

"Don't get me started on human form," I said, shaking my head. "It's awful, just awful. When May— she's the silver wyvern's mate, and a really nice chick even if she is a doppelganger—when May made me take up human form a few months ago, everyone laughed at me. I don't think I'll ever get over the trauma of that experience."

"How very odd," Anastasia said, looking me over. "I can't imagine preferring a canine form over that of a human, but I'm sure you have your reasons."

Buttercup looked sour and mean at the same time, but she kept her pie-hole shut for the trip to the airport. Until the plane took off, that is.

"Mistress?" I was curled up on a loveseat that sat along one side of the jet when Buttercup unsnapped herself from a big comfy chair and moved forward to where Anastasia was sitting with a book. "Are you all right? Mistress?"

"What's wrong with her?" I asked, hitting pause on the DVD I was watching. I slid off the seat and wandered forward, wondering if the old lady was scared of flying or something. I would reassure her that Drake's pilot was really good, and there was nothing to worry about over a quick trip to Paris.

"Mistress?"

"I think...oh dear, I don't feel well. Don't feel well at all," Anastasia said groggily. "I can't seem to keep... eyes..."

"You're having some sort of an attack," Buttercup said briskly, shaking the old lady by the shoulders. "We will get you to a doctor immediately, but Mistress, the demon! If you are unable to command it, it will do who knows what heinous acts!"

"Hey!" I said, allowing a little blop of slobber to hit her shoe nearest me. "I don't do heinous! Not when I'm on vacation, anyway!"

"Mistress, you must make an effort!" Buttercup demand.

Anastasia's eyes fluttered open, the faded blue of them cognizant but obviously sedated. A horrible, nasty suspicion filled me at the sight of her dilated pupils. "The demon...you must take charge."

"Now, wait a sec," I said, shoving my head in between them to try to sniff at Anastasia's breath. It looked to me like she'd been slipped a mickey. "No one needs to take charge of me. I'm a sixth class demon. I'm not really bad. Besides, Aisling would skin me if she found out I did anything bad—"

"I am yours to command, Mistress," Buttercup said, grabbing me by the collar and hauling me back. "Tell me what you want."

"No, listen to me—" I started to say, but the old lady's eyes rolled back in her head as she said softly, "I grant you the authority given to me."

I stared in horror first at her, then at Buttercup as she straightened up, a victorious smile on her face.

"You drugged her!" I gasped, shocked to my toenails.

"You'll have a hard time proving that where you're going," she said, then waved her hands around in a hokey manner and said quickly, "Effrijim, I command you in the name of my mistress, in the name of your Guardian, and in the name of all that is good and right in the world. I banish your unclean being to the Akasha, where you belong!"

"Noooo!" I wailed halfway through her speech, but it did no good. One second I was standing next to a comatose old lady who thought I was distinguished, and the next I was next to rocky outcropping that jutted up out of a sepia-toned landscape filled with shadows, horror, and endless torment.

CHAPTER TWO

"Welcome to the Akasha. Is this your first time here?" a chirpy voice asked. "Would you like some introductory literature?"

I leaped to my feet and realized right off the bat that something truly horrendous had happened.

"Argh!" I yelled, lifting up my arms and staring with horrified shock at five long fingers at the end of each of the two arms. "I'm in human form again!"

"You certainly are," the perky voice said, a tinge of disapproval sounding as it added, "And you seem to have misplaced your clothes—by the love the saints! Don't do that again!"

I straightened from where I had bent double to look at my feet, turning around to face the person to whom the voice belonged.

A little woman stood in front of me, one hand clapped over her eyes.

"Fires of Abaddon! I got sent to the midget section of the Akasha? I'm in human form in the midget section?"

An irritated look crossed the woman's face as she lowered her hand. "That term is offensive, and shows archaic and ignorant thinking. We prefer the term 'little people,' not that there is a little person section of the Akasha." She took a deep breath, then slapped another smile on her face, but this one looked awfully brittle. "So long as you promise never to bend over again when I am behind you, I am willing to overlook the fact that you are without clothing. Let's see, where was I? Oh, yes, here is a pamphlet that details the Akasha, including a brief history, notable members, and what you can expect over the centuries. Since you look confused, I'll give you a brief overview of the situation: the Akashic Plain, as it is more formally known, is what mortal beings think of as limbo, although in reality it's much more than that. Beings of both light and dark natures are banished here for eternal punishment without any hope of escape or reprieve."

I took the pamphlet she shoved at me. It was illustrated with faces of various beings in perpetual torment.

"The Akasha is governed by the Hashmallim, who are kind of a form of Otherworld police, although they are not bound by any rules except those of the Court of Divine Blood. Are you familiar with the Court?"

"I can't believe that rotten Butterbutt changed me into a human when she banished me. She did it on purpose, I just know she did. Of all the double-dealing…now what am I supposed to do? I can't stand around like this," I said, waving my hand toward my torso. A horrible thought struck me. I looked. "Satan's little imps! My package! It's…it's…"

The tiny little woman gave my package due consideration. "Unimpressive is the word that springs immediately to mind, and I use the word 'springs' without any innuendo whatsoever."

"Aw, man! I'm human with a short-changed knapsack!"

"Sir."

"What? Oh, yeah, I used to be a sprite," I said. "I'm familiar with the Court. So when did the Akasha get greeters?"

"A few years ago, when it was noticed that many people arrived here without a clue as to what to do next." She pursed her lips. "Some people appear to be even more clueless than others."

"Since this is the ultimate place of punishment, I figured suffering untold torments was pretty much the plan of the day," I said. "This is horrible. I can't stay like this until Aisling notices that I'm not in Paris. I gotta do something!"

"That is your own concern, sir. I should warn you that there is no way out except through intervention of the Sovereign, and it's not likely that it will bother itself with something like a sixth class demon, now is it?" She tipped her head on the side as she beamed at me. "Especially not one that insists on prancing about the Akasha in the nude. Enjoy your eternity here. Ta-ta!"

She turned and picked her way through the rocky, jarring landscape until she disappeared behind a particularly jagged piece of rock that thrust upward out of the earth as if it had burst forth by immeasurable forces.

"I'd like to ta your ta, sister," I muttered. "Great. Just great. My first day on vacation, and I end up in the Akasha, naked, and in friggin' human form. Good thing I still have my cell phone. I'll just call Ash up and tell her she has to summon me the h-e-double hockey sticks out of here."

I picked up my backpack, and had just extricated the cell phone Aisling gave me for my last birthday, when a herd of five fur and leather-clad phantasms suddenly appeared and plowed right into me.

"Hrolf! Look! A naked demon!" One of them stopped long enough to give me the once over. "What's it got here, then?"

"Hey!" I yelled when the phantasm snatched the cell phone right out of my hand.

"A demon? 'Ere? Roll 'im, Runolf," another of the phantasm said as they continued to move onward.

"Fires of Abaddon! Give that back! And my backpack! Hey!"

Runolf the phantasm—a ghost that's been banished and has no hope of ever regaining his or her ghostly self back—stopped long enough to jeer at me. "We're Vikings, demon. We stop for no man! Or...er... demon. Yar!"

"That's pirate-speak, not Viking-speak, you idiot!" I yelled as I started after him. Here's the thing, though—phantasms come from ghosts, right? So they aren't big in the corporeal department to begin with, and once they've been phantasmed, they're even less on the whole "can touch things in the plain of reality" scale. So while they could zoom around the place like a ghostly Viking blight, those of us bound to physical forms had to fight our way through a landscape that brought new meaning to the phrase "cut the your feet to ribbons." They were out of sight in a matter of a couple of seconds.

"Ow. Ow ow ow. Ow. Son of a sinner! Now I have a rock shard stuck between my toes!"

I sat down and yelped, leaping up immediately. "What the—ass skewers? This is worse than Abaddon!" I moved over to a spot that was mostly free of sharp, rocky spikes, and plopped down to suck on my sore toes. "Man, this is supposed to be my vacation. Not having fun! I wanna go home."

"At least you have a vacation," a voice spoke behind me. "I haven't had any such thing in…oh, it must be seventy years now."

I peered over my shoulder, eyeing the woman who perched on a rock behind me. "It ain't much of a vacation, sister. Who're you?"

"My name is Titania," the woman said, giving me one of those sultry-eyed once-overs that nymphs were so known for. "You're naked. You're a demon and you're naked."

"Yeah, and you're a nymph. I didn't know they sent you guys to the Akasha. I thought they just ripped off your wings or beat you with your halo if you did something bad."

She made a face. "You're thinking of faeries. They are the wicked ones. If I ever catch that bastard, lying, two-timing Oberon, I shall show him that he can't just throw me away like this. I have rights, too, you know!"

"Titania, huh? What do your friends call you for short? Titty?" I snickered to myself.

She straightened up and gave me a look that would have melted my guts if I weren't a demon. "They call me Titania!"

"Gotcha. Wait a sec...Oberon? Titania?" I kicked my brain into high and dug through some old memories. "Midsummer's Night Dream?"

"Pfft." She examined a rose-tipped fingernail. "That Will Shakespeare got it all wrong. He said I was a faery. As if! He totally dissed us nymphs, and let me tell you, the nymphhood was not happy about that."

"Yeah, I heard you guys can be kind of...eh... militant," I said, wondering if she wanted to use those long nails to hit all my scritchy spots. Then I remembered I didn't have scritchy spots. At least, not in this repulsive form. I glared at my package.

"What on earth are you doing?" she asked.

"Glaring at my crotch. A Guardian did this to me," I said, mourning the loss of my fabulous doggy form.

She, too, stared at my groin. "She has a lot to answer for."

"You said it. I wish I could do something to pay her back. Hey! Nymphs! You guys are all militant and badass, right? I could have some of your buddies beat up the Guardian who screwed me over."

"We prefer the term proactive to militant,." Titania pulled out a nail file and tended to a fingernail. "And if you had spent your life as underestimated and overlooked as we have been, you'd be proactive about making sure people got their facts right, too."

"I'm a demon," I answered, carefully sitting down and examining my abused foot. "I am all over underestimated."

"Anyway, Shakespeare got it all wrong," she continued. "Oberon isn't king of the faeries at all. He's just an advocate for the Court of Divine Blood."

"Advocate? Like a lawyer?"

"An obscenely vile one, yes."

"Yeah? So what did you do that you got tossed in here?" I asked.

"Oberon, my former lover, and disgusting lint in the underbelly of the worst sort of beings, decided to dump me, a priestess in the house of Artemis, for a naiad. Can you believe it? He dumped me for a water trollop!" Her expression went from outraged to calculating in a split second. "But he'd just better watch out, because the minute I'm out of here, I'm going to get my pound of flesh."

"Ew," I said, wrinkling my nose. "Wait—a human pound of flesh, or meat from, oh, say, the rump of a corn-fed Black Angus cow? Because the latter sounds really good right about now. Especially with a whisky barbecue sauce."

"If I could just find a way out, I could rally the sisters and we'd have our revenge!"

"On who, Shakespeare? Got news for you, babe. He's dead."

"No, not him. Oberon."

I thought. I always think better sitting down. "Not that I want to rush you, since I've got at least ten days before Aisling comes back from her cruise and finds out that witch on two legs drugged her boss just so she could banish me, but I'm a bit confused. I get that boy toy dumped you in here when he was hooking up with a naiad, but how does that translate to you nymphs going to war against him?"

"He's Oberon," she said, just like that made sense. When I scrunched up my face in an attempt to figure that out, she added, "He didn't just have me banished to the Akasha—he had all nymphs banished from the Court in order to curry favor for his own kind."

"Oh, yeah," I said, dredging up a memory. "I think I remember reading something about that. You guys got run out of town because you were causing all sorts of trouble."

"We did nothing of the sort. Oberon just made it look like we did," she said, leaping to her feet and shaking her fist at the air. "He will pay for that! He will pay for…" Her words suddenly stopped.

I lifted an eyebrow in a move just as smooth as the one Drake makes whenever Aisling says something outrageous.

"You're a demon," she said.

"You got that right, baby cakes. Sixth class," I said, winking. "But if you were interested in hooking up with me, I gotta tell you that I'm in a relationship right now with a Welsh Corgi named Cecile. She has the cutest little fuzzy butt you ever did see."

She stared at me just like I said something weird.

"You're a demon," she repeated. "Thus, you can get me out of here."

"If I could get anyone out of here, it would be me, because I have a score to settle with a conniving apprentice Guardian, but I can't, so I won't."

"Yes, you can. You're a creature of Abaddon. You can't be dictated to by the Court. That means you can get out."

"The Court doesn't have any say over me, but I've been sent here, in a roundabout way, by my demon lord. I can only get out if she summons me, and she's not going to know what that witch Butterfat did until she gets back and finds out I'm not with Amelie or Anastasia."

"There has to be another way!"

"Well, yeah, the Hashmallim guarding the door could let me out, but that's never happened, so it's not worth thinking about."

"Oh!" she said, stamping her foot and pointing to a spot in the distance. "Don't you dare cross me, demon! I will make your life a living hell if you don't get me out of here!"

"Look, sister, I just said—"

"Do it!" she bellowed.

Thirty hours later I gave in to her gigantic ongoing hissy fit, and headed over to the circle of Akasha, the center of the whole place, where three Hashmallim stood guard over the entrance. It was an ugly spot, like the rest of the Akasha, nothing but sharp jagged rocks with dead-looking scrubby plants that were the same shade of sepia as the dirt.

"Hi guys," I said as I got up to the nearest Hashmallim. If you've never seen one of these guys, they're Freak City with a capital Freak. They look like something that Jim Henson would have dreamed up after a night of hitting the opium pipe—tall and gaunt figures draped in black, but not really black, some sort of living black that moved and shifted, and oh yeah—they had no faces. Seriously freaky. "How they hangin'? Er…that's assuming you have any to hang. So, this nymph named Titania and I were wondering if we could get out of Dodge. She's got some vengeance thing, and I want to give a trainee Guardian what for."

The Hashmallim didn't say anything. He just stood there and stared at me. Kind of. If he'd had eyes he would have been staring me down. Then again, maybe he was looking at my package. "Now, I know you guys have rules and everything, so Titty and I—"

"Don't call me Titty!" came the echo of a roar that rolled down from a nearby rocky hilltop.

"We are happy to make it worth your while, if you know what I mean," I said, dropping my voice so the other Hashmallim couldn't hear. "I've got a credit card. Well, OK, it's actually Aisling's that she lets me use on TV shopping channels, but still, I know her pin number—I can pull out a wad of cash big enough to choke a behemoth. So what'cha say? Shall we talk turkey?"

The Hashmallim stood there and said nothing. The bastard.

By the time I ran through everything that Titania and I could think of to offer as a bribe—up to and including her sexual favors, and a sweater woven from hair brushed from my gorgeous coat—two hours had passed, and we were still no closer to getting out.

"Look, I don't want to get tough with you. I will if I have to, but you can trust me on this, it won't be pretty."

The Hashmallim remained silent, but it was a mocking kind of silence, the kind that just dared me to try him.

So I did.

It took three days, but eventually, the Hashmallim cried mercy, and opened a rend in the fabric of time and space, shoving Titania and me through it.

"Do not return," it said in its creepy, wheezy voice, then slammed shut the rend. "And do not ever sing that song again!"

"That was brilliant," Titania said, her eyes giving me a long, considering look. "I would have never thought that singing the same song for seventy hours straight would be enough to break a Hashmallim, but you did it. What exactly was that song?"

"My Humps. Effective, huh?"

"Extremely so. I thought the last time when you wiggled your butt on the Hashmallim and asked him what he was going to do with his junk that he was going to scream. Well done, demon. Very well done." She rubbed her hands and looked around the busy city street we had been dumped out on. It was Helsinki (per Titania's request), and although it was close to midnight, there were a surprising number of people wandering around. Several of them gave me an odd look.

"What's wrong, you never seen a naked demon?" I asked a woman who stopped and stared.

She looked startled and hurried off.

"OK, I fulfilled my part of our bargain—now it's your turn. You gotta get me to Paris pronto so I can salvage something of my vacation before Aisling gets back."

"A nymph always honors her promises," Titania said, grabbing my wrist and hauling me after her down the sidewalk. "But first, revenge!"

CHAPTER THREE

It turns out they have laws in Helsinki about people walking around the city buck naked. Tweny-four hours after I was arrested, Titania bailed me out of jail, and shortly after that we were on a train headed for a small town in the countryside where she assured me her ex would be celebrating

"He always loved this area for juhannus," she explained as the countryside whizzed past us. It was night, but because of the midnight sun thing that happened in the far north, it wasn't dark out at all. "We celebrated it here for centuries, so I'm certain he'll be here. The nymphood is on their way, so we'll—what's wrong?"

I squirmed in the seat. "It's my codpiece. I don't think it fits."

She rolled her eyes. "Look, you said you wanted some clothes so you wouldn't be arrested again, and I got you some clothes. I'm sorry if it's not what you like, but there's no time to go shopping for you. We have to get out to the juhannus so we can smite Oberon."

"Did you have to go shopping at a leather fetish store?" I asked, squirming again so I could adjust the leather thong, that, along with a fishnet tank top and the metal studded codpiece, made up what Titania referred to as clothing. "You couldn't have gotten me something from the Gap? There wasn't a Polo store around?"

The look she gave me resembled ones Aisling had been known to send my way. "If you have quite finished, demon, I am trying to explain to you what will happen."

"You don't have to, I was eavesdropping when you were on the phone in that leather shop. You called up your nymph buddies, and you intend to blow into your ex's party and beat the crap out of him. It's not very complicated."

"Perhaps not, but it will be delicious," she said, almost purring. Kind of like how a tiger purrs before it pounces.

"So where does the part come in where you get me to Paris?" I asked, trying to adjust the codpiece. "Man, it's bad enough I have a sub-standard package. This thing is squashing everything together into one blob. Here, take a look and see if the blood has been cut off to it."

She held up a hand to stop me from unstrapping the codpiece. "I do not have time to examine your genital blobs. Oberon is a master of manipulation. We must plan our attack down to the smallest detail."

I sighed and slumped back in the seat, listening with only half my attention as she detailed her plans.

Two hours later we met up in a park with the local nymphs that she had rallied, ready to set off on motorbikes to a campsite located on a small lake in a northern region of Finland.

"Let the world hear of the Nymph Offensive!" one of them called, donning a pair of brass knuckles.

"Nymphs unite! Together we shall challenge Oberon and his fae followers, and show them that we are a force to be reckoned with!" Titania yelled, standing on a box. "We will have vengeance for all those centuries of abuse! At long last, we shall prove our worth! Let there be no quarter for the faeries! They will know once and for all the true glory that is the nymphhood!"

The thirty or so nymphs who had managed to get to Finland on a day's notice yelled their support, shaking their fists and various weapons they had acquired. Some of the nymphs slapped on wrist guards and knuckle protectors; other brandished heavy-duty walking sticks. One waved what looked like a toilet plunger.

"But..." One of the nymphs, the one nearest me, looked at me doubtfully. "But we are not all nymphs."

All thirty women considered me. If I'd been in my normal form, I would have asked for belly scritches. But somehow, I had a feeling these babes wouldn't take that request well. I'm perceptive that way.

"Jim is just here because I owe him a boon for my release," Titania said slowly. "He is not really one of us."

"The Titster speaks the truth," I said, nodding. "I'm just here to hang out until she's creamed her ex, then she's going to get me to Paris."

The nymphs frowned at me. I started to edge away. One nymph frowning wasn't much to think about—

thirty of them, armed and annoyed at men in general, were another matter. "Sorry, did I say Titster? I meant her high and gracious nymphness, Titania the Uber."

"We cannot have a non-nymph in a Nymph Offensive," one of the chicks said, frowning some more at me.

"Hey, I'm happy to stay back and let you guys kick serious faery butt," I said, plopping down on the grass. "I'll just stay here and wait for you guys to get done, 'K?"

"You must come with us," Titania said in a huffy voice. "We had a deal. You said you would help me seek my revenge on Oberon. You must do that, or I will not aid you in returning to Paris."

"Yeah, well," I twanged my codpiece, "I ain't no nymph, and if you have a rule that only nymphs can go along to whoop-ass, then it's not gonna happen."

"We can make him an honorary nymph," the frowny chick said.

Titania looked thoughtful as all the other women voiced their approval of this plan. "I don't see why that wouldn't work. Although he must change his form into that of a female."

"No way, sister," I said, backing up. "I don't even like human form, but there's no way in Abaddon you're going to get me to change into a girl."

"Why not?" Titania asked, narrowing her eyes as she stalked toward me. "Do you have something against women?"

"Like that's even possible? It's just not a good idea for me to take on girl form. 'Cause if I did, all I'd do is jump up and down and watch my boobs bounce."

The nymphs stared at me with accusation in their eyes.

"Not like I've ever done that or anything," I added quickly, then cleared my throat. "So! Men. They're scum, right? Let's go beat up Ti-Ti's boyfriend."

Titania made me ride on her motorcycle after that, in order, she said, to save the nymphs from my lust. They made me an honorary nymph, however, which I hope Aisling never hears about, because my life will be one long pun if she does.

We got the campsite where the faeries were celebrating midsummer an hour or so later. I knew it had to be the right place because not only were there a bunch of bonfires, there were also Renaissance Faire-ish chicks wandering around in long, gauzy dresses, with garlands of flowers in their hair. That, and everyone present was a faery.

"Look at them," snarled Titania from where the Nymph Offensive was hidden behind several trees circling the lakeside camp spot. "Just look at how they fling themselves around the bonfires as if they, and not we, were beings of the earth!"

"They really do bring new meaning to the word 'frolic', don't they?" I asked, watching the faeries dance like monkeys on crack around the bonfires. "Hey, you can see right through those gauzy dresses when the light is behind them. Hoobah."

"They think they are chosen because Oberon has had us cast out of grace," Titania sneered, "but we will not stand for this any more!"

"We are of the earth! We will take back what is ours!" Frowny Nymph said. "We will rule midsummer as we were meant to rule it!"

"There will be no quarter for faeries!" Titania said, accepting a long, thin sword from one of the other nymphs. She held it aloft as if it was a beacon. "We will take no prisoners! We will have no mercy!"

"Babe, just between you and me, I think you've seen Lord of the Rings one time too many times," I said, leaning toward her so everyone wouldn't overhear. "Viggo, you ain't. If you want my advice—"

She didn't. "This is war, my sisters!" she interrupted me, waving her sword toward the innocent faeries tripping the firelight fantastic. "It is them or us! All I ask is that you leave that lying traitor Oberon for me! Nymphhood—arise!"

On that battle cry, the group of women charged forward, causing immediate panic in the frolicking faeries. They ran screaming away from us, hands waving in the air as they raced around like winged Ren-Faire clad chickens, bumping into each other, the air thick with spurts of faery dust.

It was chaos, sheer chaos, and although one of the nymphs shoved a rake in my hand before she charged off, wielding a chunk of garden hose like it was nunchuks, I stayed in the back and tried to keep out of the way of maddened nymphs.

"Nice...er...wings," I said as one flower-bedecked faery in a translucent gown ran past me screaming at the top of her lungs, a nymph in hot pursuit. I wandered over to where two other nymphs had a male faery pinned, and were taking turns beating him over the head with a bouquet of flowers he'd evidently strapped to his hip (male faeries aren't, as a rule, the Otherworld's most manliest men). "Two against one—I like your style," I told the nymphs, giving them a thumb's up as I moved past.

It didn't take long for the nymphs to wreak complete havoc amongst the fae folk. Ten minutes after they charged in, the whole motley gang of faeries were huddled together in one glittery, gauzy group. Muffled sobs and murmurs of comfort were periodically heard, but they gave the nymphs who stood over them, brandishing their weapons, no further problem.

None of them did except the head faery, that is. Titania had squared off with her ex next to the biggest bonfire, a big blond dude with feathered hair and a garland of ivy leaves on his head. "There you are!"

"Titania! My love! My darling! My one true...er... one! How I have missed you!"

"You lying bastard!" Titania said as she marched around him. Two of the nymphs held his arms while she circled him, the sword pointed right at him. He looked worried. "You missed me? You're the one who had me banished to the Akasha, just so you could screw some watery naiad!"

"That was all a mistake. It was a glamour! Nothing more! She temporarily deranged my mind, but as soon as I came out of it and realized what she had forced me to do, I moved heaven and earth to get you out and back to my arms, my dearest, loveliest Titania."

"Which explains why you had all nymphs cast out of the Court, eh?" Titania asked making another circuit around him. This time she poked him here and there with the tip of the sword. She didn't actually draw blood, but he jumped each time the point touched him.

"It was the glamour!" he said, starting to sweat. "I swear to you, I would never have done anything to harm you or your girls—"

The sword poked deep enough into his skin to leave a drop of blood glowing on its tip.

Oberon squawked. "Ladies, I mean ladies! I would never do anything to harm you or your ladies! You know that, my dearest, darling. I live for you, my love. My heart beats for you, only for you. Take my crown, take my wings, take everything away from me—everything but your love."

"Aw, man, I feel that chili dog I had for dinner coming back on me," I said, rubbing my belly. "You don't think you could lay it on a little more thick, do you, bud? I bet another round of you telling Tittles how much you love her would have me refunding."

Oberon's eyes flashed at me for a second before he made puppy dog eyes at Titania.

"A glamour, you say." Titania stopped in front of him, her eyes assessing what she saw.

"It had to be that, my darling, my beauteous one. You know I have devoted my whole life to you."

I didn't believe it, but evidently Titania fell for it. She lowered her sword and allowed Oberon to scoop her up in his arms, murmuring all sorts of lovey-dovey crap that anyone with half a mind could tell was total bull.

"I think I really may ralph," I told the nearest nymph, the one who frowned so much. She looked a bit green around the gills, too. "Hey, Ti! You gonna get me to Paris before you and the Obster there go off to the land of Boinksville?"

"Certainly. Cobs, take the demon to the portal in Helsinki, and see that it's sent to Paris. Now, Oberon, about the repeal on the ban of nymphs at the Court…"

The pair of them wandered off. "How long do you give that?" I asked the nymph named Cobs as she gestured for me to follow her. The other nymphs were releasing the wad of damp faeries, all of whom twitched whenever one of the nymphs came too close.

"Oberon is a smart man. I doubt if he'll cross Titania again. Especially after he sees what she's brought with her," she said, nodding as another nymph carrying a box ran past us toward Titania.

"Really? Why, what's in the box?"

She smiled as she swung a leg over her motorcycle. "Wing clippers."

CHAPTER FOUR

"Paris at last!" I said as I got to my feet. Portalling is never easy on the bones, although most portal companies have wised up and put a stack of padding at the recipient portal, so at least you don't actually break anything when you arrive. "Ow. Think I pulled my spleen or something. Still, Paris at last! Hold on Cecile, daddy is on his way!"

The chick at the portal company's desk barely even looked up from her magazine as I gave her a cheery grin before I headed out the door. I stopped on the doorstep, breathing deeply of the diesel-laden, slightly smoggy, damp and mildew-smelling air of Paris that I knew and loved. "Paris at last," I repeated happily, then took one step down to the street, and was promptly grabbed by a couple of strong-armed thugs, and tossed into the back of an unmarked black van.

"Fires of Abaddon!" I shouted into someone's armpit. I didn't see whose until I was rudely shoved backward with a word that the speaker should have been ashamed of. "What the...hey! Don't I know you?"

"Get off me!" The woman who was on the floor of the van kicked out at me as she got to her feet and took a seat on the bench that ran along one side of the van. "Effrijim! I thought I detected the stench of a demon."

"Ow! No kicking the codpiece! Until I get put back into my normal form, this package is all I have. Anyen? What in the name of Bael's ten toes are you doing here? I thought you ghedes only hung out in the Caribbean. What are you doing in Paris?"

"What do you think I am doing?" Anyen answered. She was tall and thin, her skin as black as midnight, dressed in a long black coat and wearing black glasses, and possessing a very cool Haitian accent. "I'm here to collect revenants, of course. We're building an undead army, and it's impossible to do that in Haiti anymore. Ever since that damned Internet became popular, everyone knows how to protect themselves from us. It's almost more than a decent, hard-working soul-stealer can bear, let me tell you!"

She sniffled just like she was going to cry, but everyone knew ghedes couldn't cry. It had something to do with their origins.

"Yeah, well, life's tough all over. Take mine, for instance," I said, pulling myself up to the opposite bench. The van we were in had a solid wall between the cargo and driver's area, but judging by the motion, I gathered we were en route to somewhere. "One minute I'm on vacation, about to see the love of my life, and the next—whammo. It all goes to Abaddon. Who nabbed us, do you know?"

She spat out a word that I figured wasn't very nice. "That new Venediger. I heard that she was cleaning up

Paris, kidnapping innocent beings just because we have dark origins. She has squads of her minions watching the portal shops, abducting anyone she doesn't deem fit to be in the mortal world. It is outrageous, a violation of my rights, and I shall most definitely be complaining to the Akashic League about it! Only they have the right to hold a ghede, and they would not be so foolish to do so."

"Oh, the Venediger," I said, relaxing. "Jovana. No sweat, then. We're old buds, we are. My demon lord helped put her in power. I'm sure once she knows it's me her goon squad picked up, she'll have me released."

Anyen made a face like she didn't believe me at all, and said nothing more till we arrived at a hoppin' nightclub named Goety and Theurgy.

"Ah, G&T," I said as the two guys who nabbed me hauled me inside the club. Two others emerged to bring Anyen. "Brings back old memories. Hey, there's a buffet here now? Can we swing by it? I'm starving."

The bully-boys didn't stop. They just hauled me past the buffet, past the dance floor, and down a dimly-lit flight of stairs to equally dimly-lit basement.

"Guys? The V is an old buddy of mine. You might want to tell her that it's me you have, so she doesn't get too pissed with you when she finds out you're doing this."

Neither man said anything.

"Name's Jim. Well, Effrijim, really, but that's kinda girly, so I just go with Jim. Jovana knows me."

They still didn't say anything. They hauled me across the basement, and without one single word, dumped me into a small room, tossed Anyen in after me, and slammed the door shut.

"I will have your heads for this!" she bellowed as they locked the door. She pounded on it making all sorts of threats, but eventually she stopped and glared at me.

"Why are you looking at me like that?" I asked, kicking aside a cardboard box and plopping down on a dirty-looking cot that sat in the corner. "I didn't lock us in here."

"The Venediger is your friend. You said she was."

"Maybe they're going up to tell her who I am," I said, rubbing my sore toes. Box kicking while you're barefoot isn't the best of ideas. "Maybe they'll be back all groveling and with plates of buffet food in an attempt to curry favor with me. Oooh, curry. Devils and demons, am I hungry."

"That doesn't help me any," she said in a rather surly tone. "It is your duty to get me out of here."

"Sorry, sister, not again. I just went through one big escape scene—I'm not going to do another. Not for a really long time. I don't think I could stand to sing about my lady lumps one more time."

Anyen turned her back on me, but only after she lit me up one side and down another. It's a good thing I'm immortal, or those curses she'd been flinging at me might have done some damage.

"I'm going to die of hunger. I'm going to starve to death. When Aisling finally tracks me down, she's going to find nothing but a skeleton left," I complained a good eighteen hours later. "You think this mattress is edible?"

Anyen, who had kicked me off the mattress and claimed it for her own, rolled over just long enough to glare at me. I was about to point out that I would share it with her when the noise of a key in the lock had me leaping to my feet. "Yay, Jovana finally heard I was here and she's going to let me out! That or they're going to bring us some food. Either works for me."

"The Venediger wishes to see you," one of the bully-boys said as he opened the door.

I blinked in the relatively bright light. "Yeah, I figured she'd want to make her apologies to me in person," I said, sauntering nonchalantly out of the room. "Can we stop by the buffet first? I'm about to faint with hunger."

"Effrijim!" Anyen belted out my name so it had the force to send me reeling a few steps. "I will not be left here! You must take me with you!"

I thought for a moment about telling her to suck it up—I am a demon, after all—but I was feeling generous, so I nodded toward her and asked the nearest guard, "Anyen wants to come with. You don't mind, do you?"

The guard shrugged. "She may come as well, although the Venediger will not be ready for her until tomorrow."

"Told ya the V was my good friend," I said to Anyen as she shoved me out of the way, jerking her arm out of the guard's hand. She stalked in front of me, tossing her head once, and saying merely, "We shall see."

We weren't led into the bar proper—which was closed, since it was now early morning—but into one of the back rooms. It was some sort of a conference room, with a long table that had been draped with a black cloth, and three people who stood talking quietly in a small clutch.

THE PERILS OF EFFRIJIM

"Hey, nice to see ya again," I said, waving at the woman to whom the other two looked the second I stepped in the door. She was small, well-dressed, and had a pageboy haircut that always made Aisling giggle. "I see you're still going in for those power suits, huh?"

Jovana, once a mage and now the person in charge of the Otherworld in Europe, aka the Venediger, stared at me as if I had an extra testicle.

"Oh, man, you don't recognize me, do you? Yeah, the human form is a bit awkward, huh? But it's really me, Jim. Aisling's demon. You probably remember me in Newfie form. Big black dog, luxurious coat, package that would do a pony proud. Remember now?"

"Take the sacrifice to the table," she said, waving toward me before turning her back on me to fuss over something behind her.

"Oooh, breffies?" I said, hurrying forward. "I'm starved...hey! Sacrifice?"

The two burly dudes grabbed me by either arm and jerked me up onto the table. When Jovana turned back toward me, she held a wavy bladed silver dagger in her hand. I had a really awful feeling I knew just what she was planning on doing with it. "Fires of Abaddon! You're nuts, lady!"

"Silence!" she commanded, and gestured toward one of the flunkies standing against the wall.

A man came forward, pulled out a scroll, and read. "Demon of unknown origins found arriving via portal in the Latin Quarter on Tuesday afternoon."

"Jim," I said quickly, eyeing that nasty dagger. "My name is Jim!"

"You are charged with violation of the Roaming Demon Ordinance of 2008."

"What?" I squawked, trying to squirm out of the two thugs' grip. "What Roaming Demon Ordinance?"

"In accordance with the laws sanctified by the Venediger, your mortal form will be destroyed, and your being sent back to Abaddon where you belong."

"You can't do that!" I yelled, watching as the Venediger nodded and a Guardian came forward, pulling out a gold stick and beginning to scribe a circle around me. "Aisling is going to be really pissed!"

The Guardian paused, looking up. I'd never seen her before, but evidently she'd heard of Ash. "Aisling? Aisling Grey?" she asked.

"Yeah, that's her. Aisling is my boss." I craned my neck to glare up at Jovana. "The same person who gave you your job!"

Jovana narrowed her eyes on me for a few seconds. "It is true that Aisling Grey has a demon under her control. But I have heard that the demon's preferred form is that of a dog."

"Man alive, doesn't anyone listen to me?" I complained, trying to pull my arm free.

Jovana nodded to the guard, who let go of me. I yanked my hand free from the other one and sat up, rubbing my wrists. "I just got done telling you that I'm normally in dog form, but another Guardian ordered me into human form because she knew it would tick me off."

Six pairs of eyes considered me as I slid off the table to my feet. I straightened my codpiece, dusted off my leather thong, and raised an eyebrow while I waited for the apologies to flow.

The Guardian rose from where she'd been kneeling. "If this demon speaks the truth—"

"I may be a lot of things, but I've never been a liar," I said grumpily.

"If it speaks the truth, then I want no part of this," she continued, putting away her gold stick. "Aisling Grey is one of the most powerful Guardians in the Guardians' Guild. She is a savant, especially gifted, and someone I do not wish to cross."

"Anyen will tell you who I am," I said, waving at the ghede.

She glared back at me.

"Hey, I helped you, now it's time for you to repay me," I told her.

"Oh, very well. The demon does not lie. It is Effrijim. I have known it for several centuries," she said, albeit kinda grudgingly.

"There, see? All's well," I said, heading for the door. "I'll tell Ash you send her love, 'K? See ya round."

"Halt!" the Venediger said, and instantly the two guards were in front of the door, their eyes narrow little slits as they frowned at me. "I do not accept this foul thing's statement."

"Foul thing!" Anyen said, starting forward. I grabbed her before she could jump the Venediger. "I am not a—"

"Hackles down," I said softly. "Now isn't the time unless you want to get us both tossed back into that cell in the basement."

"That is exactly where you are going," the Venediger said, putting down the dagger. She looked at it regretfully for a moment before pinning me back with a glare that stripped the hair from my toes. "You will remain there until I can speak with the Guardian Aisling Grey to verify your identity."

"No way!" I protested. "I've got…let me count… man, I've only got one day left of my vacation. I'm not going to spend it sitting in that room with a pissed off ghede!"

"Nor will I go back to that squalid little room!" Anyen declared.

"Fine." Jovana shrugged. "Then we will perform your release ceremony now. There will be no Guardian to object to you being sent back to Abaddon, I trust."

Anyen's eyes opened up really wide when the Venediger picked up the dagger again.

"You know what?" I asked Anyen, taking a deep breath and thinking about Cecile's warm, furry little ears.

"What?" she asked.

"We're immortal."

She blinked at me for a second, but that's all I gave her. I grabbed her arm, lowered my head, and charged the Venediger. She sprang to the side, out of the way, just as I figured she would. Anyen and I kept going through, right past the Venediger, the two others staring at us in surprise, and on through the window that opened onto a small garden.

Anyen was fast on her feet, luckily, and although my chest and arms and legs were cut by the glass as I went through the window, we both landed on our feet, and took off running.

The Venediger's guards, however, were mortal, and they were less than thrilled about leaping into a mass of broken glass. They were slower getting through the window, and by the time they got to the garden, we were racing down the back alley and freedom.

We split up not long after, Anyen making a snarky remark about me slowing her down.

"You're welcome," I yelled after her as she disappeared into the Tuilleries. "Hope you don't get a really nasty case of zombie rot while you're raising the dead!"

It took me a couple more hours before I finally lost the guard who persisted in following me, so it wasn't until afternoon that I staggered exhausted, bleeding, and dirty from a fall into the Seine, through the door of a familiar shop. "Cecile! Baby! I'm here!"

The woman behind the counter at the shop stared at me in stark surprise. "Jim? Is that you?"

"Hiya Amelie. Yeah, it's me. Where's Cecile?"

"She…she…" Amelie seemed to be struck speechless because she simply pointed upstairs.

"Thanks. Mind if I use your shower? I had a run in with the Venediger and I'm all ooky with blood and stuff. See you later," I called as I dashed through the back room, then up the stairs that led to the apartment in which Amelie and Cecile lived.

Cecile was also a bit taken aback by my appearance, her eyes going even more bug-eyed than they normally were when I scooped her up in my arms and kissed her all over her adorable pointy little snout. "My darling, my adorable one! We might only have one day left together, but I will make it a day you won't forget. I promise I'll get back to my normal form as soon as possible," I told her when she tried to squirm out of my hold, her little stubby legs kicking wildly. "This one sucks big time, huh? Don't worry, my beloved. I'll soon be your big, handsome Jim again. But first, a shower."

The sound of voices drifted in to me when I stepped out of the shower, drying myself on one of Amelie's soft towels. I looked at the codpiece and thong, but decided I just couldn't wear them any longer. By the time I headed out of Amelie's bedroom, I realized that I knew the voices.

"—came back early because Drake insisted on seeing the doctor. It turned out to be nothing, of course, just a case of the sniffles."

"Any illness in infants can be serious," Drake's voice rumbled in response. "I was not easy in my mind until the children had been seen by a proper doctor."

"Anyway, we decided it wasn't worth hauling the babies back to the yacht, so we figured we'd just swing by and pick up Jim and head back to London. Is it here?"

"Aw, man!" I said, marching in to the room. "You're early? Fine! Just ruin my plans!"

The silence that greeted my arrival in Amelie's sunny living room was thick enough to cut with a butter knife.

"Er…" Amelie said, her expression kind of shocked.

"Jim! What on earth are you doing in that form!" Aisling demand, her hands on her hips. "And naked!"

Drake narrowed his green eyes at me and muttered something about knowing better than to leave me on my own.

"It's not my fault," I told them both. "You can ask that no good, conniving Guardian why I'm like this."

"I certainly will," Aisling said, staring.

Drake slapped his hand over her eyes and glared at me. "Put some clothing on, or I'll see to it you have nothing left with which to shock Aisling."

She giggled.

"I don't want to wear clothing! I want my old form back. Let me change back, Ash. Please."

"All right, you can change into your normal form," she said, giggling again. "But I want to hear everything that happened. Only not right now—we had a message from Nora when we got to Drake's house."

I sighed with relief as I shifted back to my fabulous Newfoundland form, making a quick check to be sure everything was the way I had left it. "Boy, did I miss you, tail. And package. And four paws. And—"

"Enough," Drake said, bowing to Amelie. "You will excuse us if we leave in haste. Aisling is anxious to get back to London."

"Yes, I am. Come on, Jim! There's work to be done," Aisling said in her chipper voice as she took Drake's hand. "Nora said there's been a huge outbreak of kobolds and imps and all sorts of nasties in the last few days, and she's overwhelmed and needs our help in cleaning everything up. It'll be like old times tackling them together, huh?"

"Oh, man," I said, covering my face with my paws. "Can't I just sleep here for a couple of days? Cecile and I—"

"Don't be silly," she said, cuffing me on the shoulder. "You've had ten days together; that's long enough. Besides, there's nothing like a bit of action after a nice long, relaxing vacation to get your blood pumping again, now is there?"

KATIE'S GUIDE TO ALL THINGS DRAGONS

BLACK DRAGON SEPT

The black dragons have had a tremendous impact on the weyr, both in the past and present. One of the original four septs to be created at the bidding of the First Dragon, the black sept was comprised mostly of dragons living in the Baltic and Russian regions of Western and Eastern Europe.

The most famous member of the sept is also the most infamous: the dread wyvern Baltic, who was named heir to Alexei Istomka after he challenged and beat the existing heir. Baltic took over as wyvern in 1212, and was the original target of what came to be known as the Endless War when the wyvern of the red dragon sept declared an all-out war against the black dragons. Since the black dragons were, at that time, defending themselves from attacks by the blue sept, a weyr-wide war was not long in forming.

Baltic's handling of the black dragons during the Endless War was cited as Constantine Norka's reason for leaving the black dragons and forming the silver sept. As the war progressed, the black dragons began to focus more on reclaiming the silver sept, but that goal was lost when the war was brought to an end at the beginning of the 18th century with the death of Baltic at the hands of his heir, Kostya Fekete. With the black dragon stronghold, Dauva, destroyed, and most of the sept dead, the few remaining black dragons went into hiding, emerging only recently with the reappearance of the current wyvern.

Current Wyvern: Konstantin Nikolai Fekete (Kostya)
Born: 1 January 1584
Mother: Doña Catalina de Elférez
Father: Cziriak Toldi Fekete
Siblings: one living
Mate: Aoife Dakar
Previous Wyvern: Baltic

Although dragons, as a rule, do not exhibit many abilities related to various forms of magic, the black dragons have an almost uncanny ability to do that which other septs can't: they wield a particular form of elemental magic based on their natural element, energy.

They can transform the energy they gather from the relationship between living things surrounding them, and translate it into particularly effective spells. They are also experts at deception and hiding, which is why they are seldom found if they desire to remain hidden from the prying eyes of other dragons. That ability extends to objects, which can leave their lairs and items of value extremely difficult to locate.

They are also very resilient, and although they can be killed, their ability to pull energy from their surrounding allows them to survive where other dragons would not. There is a rumor that their essence turns to pure energy when they succumb to a fatal blow.

Population: 14

BLUE DRAGON SEPT

Originally from Eastern Europe, the blue dragon sept relocated sometime around the first millennium to Italy, where the highest concentrations of members still live. The blue dragons were for centuries the weakest of all five septs, and were almost completely destroyed in the Endless War when two-thirds of the members were murdered in a brutal attack by the black dragons. The sept withdrew from both mortal and immortal socializations following the war, per the request of the Wyvern at the time.

The following century was a time for restructure and reorganization, with the blue dragons returning to active participation in the Weyr by late seventeenth century. Notable members include: Rosana Flore (the first female wyvern, later murdered by her brother in 1318), Alberti Da Ghiacceto (who is said to have created the recipe for the dragon's blood beverage), and Bastiano Blu, uncle of the current wyvern, who was unsuccessful three times in his attempt to take control of the sept. He went insane shortly after the last attempt, and is rumored to be living in a remote villa in the Italian Alps.

With Bastian's coup in taking over control of the sept, members divided themselves into camps that followed either Bastian or his nephew Fiat.

Current Wyvern: Bastiano de Girardin Blu
Born: 1 January 1413, Firenze, Italy
Mother: Cecilia Mocenigo
Father: Giustiniano Tiepolo

Siblings: two
Mate: none
Took control of the sept: 2007
Previous Wyvern: Pierozzo Blu

The blue dragons are best known for two specific abilities—tracking, and telepathy. Possessors of strong social skills, they are skilled in the art of manipulation, and are renowned negotiators. They also have a keen grasp of mortal psychology, and as such, have done extremely well in businesses in the mortal world. They prefer distance fighting to hand-to-hand combat, and are fascinated with technology of any sort.

Population: 142

GREEN DRAGON SEPT

With its Celtic origins in Northern Europe, the green dragon sept has had a violent and often tragic history. Torn apart frequently by internal strife, the sept suffered from a lack of leadership for several centuries until in 1447, when the internal troubles were put to an end by the arrival of Alhazen Vireo.

A mage and mathematician, Alhazen brought stability and order to the tumultuous sept, rewriting the sept coda, and setting down rules which are kept to this day. Alhazen originally opposed participation in the Endless War, seeing no need to either claim supremacy over the other septs. When the red dragons, led by their wyvern Chuan Ren Lung, attempted to take over the sept, Alhazen reluctantly entered the war and successfully protected the sept from obliteration. Following the Endless War, Alhazen was the first to suggest a democratic structure to the weyr, with each sept receiving equal representation.

The sept again fell into confusion and disarray when Alhazen was assassinated by a red dragon. The two septs declared a private war, which waged with bloody purpose until the turn of the twentieth century, finally ending when the current wyvern agreed to a trial by combat to determine the outcome of the war. The green and red dragons have had an uneasy peace since the red dragons' defeat.

Current Wyvern: Drake Vireo
Born: 1 January 1615, Érd, Hungary
Mother: Doña Catalina de Elférez
Father: Cziriak Toldi Fekete
Siblings: one living
Mate: Aisling Grey
Took control of the sept: 1 January 1857
Previous Wyvern: Fodor Andras Vireo

The green dragons are thieves, and as such, are very adept at getting in and out of close quarters, smuggling, and upon occasion, shape-shifting. They have a natural skill with puzzles and locks, and although they are amongst the most feared fighters in the dragon world, their strengths lie in close-quarter improvised battle rather than involved strategizing.

Population: 91

RED DRAGON SEPT

The red dragons have a unique history in that one wyvern has, in effect, headed the sept for most of its existence. Although her origins are lost, it is rumored that Chuan Ren Lung was the daughter of the previous wyvern, a man she murdered along with the remaining family members in order to ensure there were no other claimants to wyvern.

Regardless of her origins, Chuan Ren Lung had an iron grip on the red dragons for more than 1500 years. It was her desire for supremacy that caused two of the three major dragon wars, including the Endless War, and the private war with the green dragons (in which more than 60 percent of the red dragons perished). Forced by lack of resources and Weyr pressure to accept peace accords, the red dragons learned to live in (relative) peace with the other septs…until the sept was all but destroyed by the demon lord Bael. A new wyvern was created to bring the sept back from extinction.

Current Wyvern: Rowan Malley Dakar
Born: 1 January 1980
Mother: Angharad Malley
Father: Alpha Ndakaaru
Siblings: Bee Dakar, Aoife Dakar
Mate: Sophea Long
Previous Wyvern: Chuan Ren Lung

The red dragons are fierce warriors, and masters of all combat arts. They believe might makes right, and lack diplomatic skills and abilities that come naturally to other septs. They have little tolerance for fools or weaknesses, and have a history of periodically purging their sept of members who don't meet their high standards. They are bold and confident, unquestioning in their loyalties to their sept, and do not hesitate to challenge anyone who stands in their path.

Note: information about the previous wyvern is provided here since the new wyvern has no history with the sept. Previous wyvern's name: Chuan Ren Lung. Born: 1 January 412, Shanxi, China. Death: 2012. Mother: Lei Su. Father: Hao Lei. Siblings: Unknown. Mate: Li Jiaxin. Took control of the sept: 1 January 670.

Population: 6

SILVER DRAGON SEPT

Not a great deal is known about the silver dragons outside the sept, due mostly to their close-knit clan, the members of which are reluctant to make public information they consider to be private business.

They are the youngest of the five dragon septs, formed when a branch from the black dragons gathered to protest the rule of the dread black wyvern Baltic, known for his ruthless and bloody attempts to dominate the five septs. The black dragons did not take kindly to their offspring leaving the sept, and spent several centuries trying to win them back—first by bribes, later by force.

The first wyvern of the silver dragons, Constantine Norka, was successful at keeping the sept autonomous, although he paid a high price for that freedom–Baltic cast a curse on the sept that promised no mate shall be born to any of its members until a black dragon was accepted as wyvern. The curse was broken in recent times.

Current Wyvern: Gabriel Tauhou
Born: 1 January 1702, Papetoai, Moorea, French Polynesia
Mother: Kaawa Savé
Father: Ra'iarii Tarapu
Siblings: 2
Mate: May Northcott
Took control of the sept: 1 January 1947
Previous Wyvern: Sial Fa'amasino

The silver dragons are renowned healers, and as such, are very much in demand in both the mortal and Otherworld. Some silver dragons also have empathic abilities, a trait that has been exploited by other septs. They have a particular affinity with nature, and many spend time with earthier beings such as wood sprites, elves, and sylphs. They are cautious and careful in battle and politics, and while they hold honor and loyalty to be among their most valued traits, they are formidable in their revenge if you cross them.
Members: 107

LIGHT DRAGON SEPT

The light dragon sept was formed when the wyvern of the black dragons was killed, and later resurrected. He then formed his own sept, which was only recently admitted to the weyr.

Current Wyvern: Baltic
Born: information missing
Mother: Maerwyn
Father: The First Dragon
Siblings: 5
Mate: Ysolde de Bouchier
Took control of the sept: 1 January 1977
Previous Wyvern: none

Baltic refuses to answer our requests for information. We suggest readers count stubbornness as one of the traits of the light dragons.

INDIGO DRAGON SEPT

The indigo sept was created by Constantine Norka upon his leaving the light dragon sept. Currently, there are only two and a half members of the sept: Constantine, his mate Bee, and a disembodied head named Gareth (honorary member, since he's not actually a dragon).

Current Wyvern
Name: Constantine Norka
Born: 1088

Mother: Elisabeth of Norka
Father: Kashi
Siblings: none
Mate: Bee Dakar
Previous wyvern: none

Constantine is very close-mouthed about the indigo dragons, but from what we can glean, they tend to be irreverent, headstrong, and single-minded. They also are soft touches when it comes to taking in strays, be it animals or people or disembodied heads.

GLOSSARY

Aisling Gray: Thirty-something mate to the Green Dragon Sept wyvern, Drake Vireo. Aisling is a Guardian (demon wrangler), and technically a demon lord since she is responsible for Jim, the demon she inadvertantly summoned in the first Aisling Gray novel. Aisling and Drake have two children.

Baltic: The dread wyvern Baltic is the first generation child of the First Dragon, the demi-god who created dragons many millenia ago. He is the former wyvern of the Black Dragon sept, which ceased when he was killed by his heir, Kostya Fekete immediately after his mate Ysolde de Bouchier was struck dead. He was recently resurrected, and found his beloved mate Ysolde (also resurrected) in the first Light Dragons book. He formed the Light Dragon Sept upon his resurrection.

Brom Sullivan: Ysolde's child by Gareth Hunt, her former husband. Brom has an unnatural interest in mummifying things, and is claimed by Baltic as his son.

Dragon heart/shards: The dragon heart is one of the most powerful artifacts on earth, and consists of five shards, which are scattered amongst the various dragon septs. The heart can be brought together and reformed, but this has only happened two times in the last millenium. Dragon shards are immensely valuable relics of the First Dragon, and thus valued beyond almost anything else.

Dragon mate: The man or woman who was born to be the mate to a dragon. Wyvern's mates are much more rare than dragon mates, and can handle and control the wyvern's fire, which would destroy an ordinary mortal.

Drake Vireo: The wyvern of the Green Dragon Sept, and a master thief. Drake has homes in London, Paris, and Budapest, and alternates his time between the three. He became a green dragon despite his black dragon father via his grandmother, who was a reeve (a special type of dragon with unusually pure bloodlines). He has two children with Aisling Gray, his mate.

Effrijim (Jim): A demon sixth class who is bound to Aisling Gray. Jim's preferred form is that of a Newfoundland dog, and he complains non-stop if he is forced into human form. Jim resides with Aisling and Drake, has a passionate love for an elderly Welsh Corgi named Cecile, who lives in Paris, and greatly enjoys eating.

First Dragon: The demi-god who created the dragonkin, he can be summoned by means of the dragon heart, or in extremely rare cases, by those who have wielded the dragon heart. As befitting a god, it's not always clear if his intentions are benevolent or not.

Gabriel Tauhou: The wyvern of the Silver Dragon Sept, and mate to May Northcott. As a silver dragon, Gabriel was cursed by Baltic to never have a mate born to him until a black dragon ruled his sept. Luckily, he found May, who as a doppelganger, was created rather than born. Gabriel has houses in London and Australia, and alternates his time between the two.

May Northcott: Doppelganger and wyvern's mate to Gabriel Tauhou. May is an identical twin to Cyrene, although she does not cast a shadow, and has no reflection in a mirror. May was formerly bound to the demon lord Magoth, and later became his consort, but was happily stripped of her title when Magoth was booted out of Abaddon. May is a shadowalker, and can slip out of the view of most people when she desires.

Savian Bartholomew: Thief-taker and tracker extraordinaire. Savian is the only person who was ever able to catch May Northcott when the L'au-dela put a price on her head. He later became a friend to both May and Gabriel, and occasionally does work for them. Husband of Maura Lo Bartholomew.

Weyr: The collection of dragon septs. The wyvern of each sept can call a sarkany, a meeting of all the wyverns, to discuss weyr business. The weyr laws govern each sept, and has diplomatic relations with the L'au-dela.

Wyvern: The leader of a dragon sept, wyverns have one human parent, and one dragon parent.

Ysolde de Bouchier: Born to the silver dragon sept some five hundred years ago, she was raised as human, and later claimed as a mate by both Constantine Norka and Baltic. She was later killed during an attack on Dauva by Constantine. She was resurrected almost immediately thereafter by the First Dragon, and spent the remaining centuries in a mental fog due to a nefarious plot by her bigamous husband Gareth. She is subjected to fugues every six months where she transmutes lead into gold. Although she appears to be human, she has a dragon self who is dormant inside her psyche. She has one son, Brom, via Gareth, and is the long-lost mate to Baltic.

DRAGON SERIES BOOKS

Aisling Grey, Guardian Novels
You Slay Me
Fire Me up
Light My Fire
Holy Smokes

Silver Dragon Novels
Playing With Fire
Up in Smoke
Me and My Shadow

Light Dragon Novels
Love in the Time of Dragons
Unbearable Lightness of Dragons
Sparks Fly

Dragon Fall Novels
Dragon Fall
Dragon Storm
Dragon Soul

Dragon Novellas
Dragon Unbound

ABOUT THE AUTHOR

For as long as she can remember, Katie MacAlister has loved reading. Growing up in a family where a weekly visit to the library was a given, Katie spent much of her time with her nose buried in a book.

Two years after she started writing novels, Katie sold her first romance, *Noble Intentions*. More than fifty books later, her novels have been translated into numerous languages, been recorded as audiobooks, received several awards, and have been regulars on the *New York Times*, *USA Today*, and *Publishers Weekly* bestseller lists. Katie lives in the Pacific Northwest with two dogs and a cat, and can often be found lurking around online.

You are welcome to join Katie's official discussion group on Facebook, as well as connect with her via Twitter, Goodreads, and Instagram. For more information, visit www.katiemacalister.com